Damaged LOCKE

(LOCKE BROTHERS, 1)

VICTORIA ASHLEY & JENIKA SNOW

Cover Designer:
Dana Leah, Designs by Dana

Cover model:
Brook Dede

Photographer:
Wander Aguiar

Proofer:
Lea Schafer

Interior Design & Formatting by:
Christine Borgford, Type A Formatting

Damaged LOCKE

1

Aston

I CLOSE MY EYES AND lean my head back as I take a long drag off my cigarette, letting the harsh smoke fill my lungs and calm my nerves.

Standing here in the blackness of the night, preparing for what the fuck my brothers and I do, never gets easier for me.

Although, I've convinced myself we do this shit for all the right reasons, some might believe we're the spawns of the fucking devil.

A blond-haired, blue-eyed evil son of a bitch to be feared.

That's what everyone sees when they look at me.

I can't say I've done much to prove them otherwise.

Whispers of the Locke brothers fill the town, facts and reality *twisted* to fit what these motherfuckers believe they know about us.

That we're sadistic bastards, incapable of any real emotions or fear.

Maybe they're not wrong about that.

My eyes open at the sound of Sterling and Ace grabbing their shit out the back of the Expedition before closing the door.

A light on across the street has my attention pulled in the wrong direction until I feel Sterling hit my arm, dragging my attention back.

"Here." He slams my sawed-off shotgun into my chest with force. "Stop holding your dick over here and take this shit."

Grinning, I yank it from his hands.

"Who wants to do the honors tonight?" Ace asks while swinging his expensive-ass titanium hammer around with pride. "Maybe Aston can just blow the damn thing down."

"I've got it, motherfuckers." Reaching into his pocket, Sterling slips on his brass knuckles and stalks up to the door, checking to see if it's locked.

It must be, because two seconds later, he's kicking the door open and walking inside as if he owns the place.

Ace flashes me a crooked smile as he pushes away from the black SUV and walks past me, running his hand over his hammer. "Put a pep in your step, baby brother. The place is wide fucking open. I call dibs on the biggest one."

Lifting a brow, I calmly make my way up the steps with my shotgun over my shoulder as Ace disappears into the house, most likely searching for some big motherfucker to take down.

And so it begins.

The dark, twisted ways of the fucking Locke brothers.

Stepping into the dirty house, I look around to see four guys inside. Four perverted, sick motherfuckers that deserve to lose their dicks and their lives for the shit they pulled last week.

These mind-fucked tweakers can't be any older than nineteen to twenty years old. A good age for them to believe they're untouchable and they can get away with taking advantage of a couple drunk girls.

Well, these dirty *untouchable* dicks are about to find out just how *touchable* they are in this town.

In our motherfucking town.

Upon noticing there's now a third person joining the party, they pull their attention away from what Ace is saying and begin shuffling to reach for weapons or whatever shit they keep hidden in this dump.

Sterling immediately swings his right fist out, connecting his fancy-ass brass knuckles to the side of one of the assholes' face, while Ace takes his hammer and places it across another guy's neck, pinning him against the wall and lifting him up it.

That leaves the other two assholes coming at me.

One of them must have *some* brains, because he drops to the ground and surrenders when he notices the gun over my shoulder.

Now the other one. Yeah . . . he's stupid as shit.

Maybe this will knock some sense into him.

Reaching into my back pocket, I pull the bandana and swing it around, the padlock busting the idiot in the eye socket, blood splattering as his face splits open.

This has the guy on the ground thinking I'm too preoccupied to see his ass get up and come toward me with a knife.

That thought gets squashed the second I pull the shotgun from my shoulder and point it at his dick, stopping him two feet from me.

"Think again, motherfucker," I growl with a tilt of my head. "On your knees. And place your hands under them . . ." I nod toward Ace. "Unless you want my brother here to show you how good he is with that hammer. He may be pretty and shit, but he's the most twisted asshole you'll meet."

He shakes his head. "No. No. I'm listening. See. Here." His bloodshot eyes stay on me, watching my gun as he lowers to the ground and drops his knife, placing his hands under his knees. "There. Can you put that away now? No one needs to get shot, bro."

I turn to Sterling to see him leaning against the couch with a smirk, one of his arms wrapped around his guy's neck to keep him in place. "These sick fuckers aren't going anywhere, little brother. Put that away . . . for now."

"All right. I guess I can do that." I smile and place the gun over my shoulder before shoving my padlock back into my pocket and kicking the dude in front of me down to the ground. That padlock really did a number on his face. "Doesn't mean your ass gets to get up." I bend down and get in his bloodied face. "Those two girls you partied with last week didn't get the option of getting up when they wanted to. Why the hell should some sick fuck like you?"

With that I kick him over to his back and dig my foot into his throat, causing him to grab at my boot and choke for air.

He struggles for a few minutes before relaxing and giving up. "We won't do it again," he manages to get out through coughs. "You're crushing my throat, man. You're going to kill my ass. We're sorry. What else do you want from us?"

I smirk, placing my hand to my ear. "What was that? I can't fucking hear you."

"We're sorry. It won't happen again. Please . . ." He struggles with pushing at my boot again, his face turning blue now as he fights to breathe. "Please don't kill me. I'm fucking begging."

Dropping my shotgun, I remove my boot from his throat and replace it with my hand, dragging him over to the couch, where I slam his head into the arm repeatedly. I don't stop until the brown fabric is covered in blood and his body goes limp. "Do it again and

I'll shoot you in the dick and then between the eyes. Got it?"

He nods his head, right before I throw him face-first down into the carpet, watching as he crawls away.

Feeling the anger completely take over me, I light up a cigarette, grab my gun, and walk outside, allowing my brothers to handle the other three assholes.

Standing here in the dark, with my hands covered in his blood, I lean against the SUV and close my eyes, attempting to calm myself down. It's not until I hear feet pounding against the sidewalk that I open my eyes and look across the street to see a woman with long black hair jogging up to the house straight across from this one.

Stopping in front of the door, she turns to face the street, her gaze landing on me.

I stand back and watch, my heart pounding like fucking mad, as she looks me over, stopping on my hands once she notices the blood.

Most people in this town would run by now. They'd hide inside their houses, peeking out the damn windows to get a glimpse of us, but not this one.

Hell no. She's standing there, taking heavy breaths as her eyes move up to meet mine.

She doesn't say anything.

She doesn't scream.

She doesn't move.

She just stands there, looking curious, as if she's using this moment to take me all in. Every damn bit of me.

I can see in her expression she knows who we are.

"Come on, Aston," Sterling calls, getting my attention away from the beautiful stranger watching me. "Get the fuck in the vehicle."

By the time I look across the street again, the woman is gone and the light that was on in the house is now off.

That must've been her bedroom light.

"Did you get the money?" I ask while backing up and reaching for the door.

"Yeah," Ace says with a crazy-ass grin. "Those fuckers were quick to throw us all their dirty money the moment I nearly crushed one of their dicks with my baby." He holds up his hammer. "These little bitches won't even be thinking about their dicks for a long time."

"Good." I toss my cigarette at the ground and jump into the SUV, my eyes seeking out the house across the street one last time.

I can't quite tell, but it looks like I see the bedroom curtain move. Apparently she hasn't gotten enough of me yet. She's braver than most people in this town, and that shit definitely has my attention.

"Let's get the fuck out of here then."

Kadence

I SUCK IN A SURPRISED breath when Melissa yanks
me into the house, slamming the door shut behind me.

"What are you doing?" She sounds worried as she rushes
through the house to shut my bedroom light off. "I warned you
about the Locke brothers the moment you moved into this town.
Are you insane, Kadence? Hell, why am I even asking that? Of
course you are."

Still fighting to catch my breath from my nightly jog, I meet
my roommate in my bedroom and reach for the water bottle on
my dresser. "You don't think *warning* me to stay away is going to
make me curious? I've waited two months to get a glimpse of these
brothers you're always going on about. I couldn't force myself to

turn away even if I wanted to, Mel. You should know me by now."

She steps away from the window and tiredly runs a hand down her face. "They're dangerous, Kadence. Everyone in this town knows it. You may be new and all, but you should take my advice and never let them see you watching them. The last thing you want is for them to know you've seen what they've done. You just witnessed a crime. Do you get that?"

The sound of the SUV starting has me rushing over to the window, pushing the curtain aside to get another peek.

It's as if I'm drawn to him, needing to see the beautiful blond stranger one more time before he disappears.

I barely get a glimpse before Melissa pulls me away and yells at me for being so careless.

"Damn it, woman." She closes her eyes and shakes her head as if she's about to lose it. "You're going to get us both killed before we even get to see our twenty-third birthdays. Not only are you insane, but you have a death wish."

"How do you even know that?" I question. "Have they ever killed anyone before? You never once told me they're murderers. All you've told me is what you hear from others around town. But has anyone actually been killed by them? Who do you know that's been hurt because of the Locke brothers? I'm sure it's not just random violence."

"No, not that I know of. I don't know, but that doesn't mean they won't start with us. The youngest Locke saw what you look like. He saw you watching him like a damn nosy person. That whole family is bad news. Everyone knows to steer clear of them. Everyone but *you*, apparently."

"Don't you think he would've marched across the street and hurt me if he wanted to? It's late at night and the whole damn neighborhood is asleep. He could've done anything he wanted to me, but he didn't. All he did was look at me as if he was curious. It was like he expected me to run away, but I didn't."

"Probably because his hands were already covered in someone else's blood and he was trying to think of ways to catch you when you're alone at a later time, damn it." She stops to catch a breath. "I about died when I looked outside to see him staring this way. It wasn't until I looked closer that I saw you standing on the porch, looking back at him."

"Those guys that live across the street . . ." I pause to take another drink of water while gazing at the curtain. "Didn't you tell me they scare the shit out of you? That they're always trying to get you alone and one of them even tried slipping something into your drink once? How do you know they haven't done that to other women?"

"I don't," she says in aggravation. "And yes, they're fucking creepy as hell and I'm scared when I see them out at night. Every girl in their right mind is. I'm not denying that, but . . ."

"Maybe the Locke brothers were there to teach them a lesson," I say, cutting her off. "Maybe they're not as bad as you all think. From what I've seen, this town is full of judgmental gossipers."

"Listen . . . the youngest Locke might look like a beautiful blond angel, but I can assure you he's as sinful and dangerous as they come." She lets out a tired breath and stops in my doorway. "*Please* just promise me you'll stay away if you see them again? I'm trying to keep you safe. You're my friend, and you wouldn't even be in this shitty little town if it weren't for me. I'm responsible for you here. I've been keeping my eye out for you since we were eight. I'm not magically stopping now, no matter how hard you fight me."

I nod my head to make her happy and ease her worry as I jump onto my bed. "All right. I get it. You've always been persistent and overprotective. It's because I love your ass so much that I followed you to this small town. Well, that and my old life sucked anyway."

She smiles slightly before speaking. "Good," she says firmly, getting serious again. "Now, good night and lock your window. I know how you like to open it after your nightly jogs, but don't. Just don't . . ."

"All right, woman. On it. Good night."

After she walks out of my room and shuts the door behind her, I immediately rush back over to the window and look outside.

My mind knows he's not out there anymore, but apparently my body didn't get the memo, because I look hard in hopes of seeing him again.

I mean face smashed against the window hard.

My eyes immediately land on one of the residents of the house across the street instead.

His face is all busted up and he's pacing across the lawn, holding something in his hand, looking extremely angry and on edge. It may be a knife.

I can't quite tell what it is, but seeing that the Locke brothers didn't leave them for dead has me completely curious what their business was with them.

I've been here for a little over two months, and I have never seen them across the street before tonight.

There's obviously something that brought them there, but what?

It wasn't to kill the creeps, and I don't see or hear any sirens heading this way to check things out.

Maybe I'll never know, and that thought is driving me crazy and making me extremely curious.

This might be a dangerous game, but I want to know about the youngest Locke brother.

If I see him again, I'm not sure I'll be able to stay away like Melissa has warned me to.

Aston

MY HANDS ARE SHAKY, MY bare skin covered in sweat as I sit here in the darkness of the basement with a cigarette resting between my tight lips.

Ever since we left that house last night, I've been slammed with visions of what I witnessed over six years ago, getting me lost in my sick, twisted mind.

No one should've had to witness the fucked-up things I saw that night, let alone a kid of only fifteen.

Nothing about me has been the same since, and with every day I die a little more inside, feeling tormented and defeated about something I had no control over.

As time passes, I begin to realize I'm stuck in my own personal hell I'll never break free of no matter how fucking hard I try.

One day, I'm afraid I'll give up altogether and just fade.

There's not much stopping that from happening.

Tensing, I step into the freezing, ice-filled water and lower myself to the bottom of the tub, hoping to chill my body temperature and distract myself from the hell in my head.

I need something else to pull me from my thoughts. Anything strong enough to keep me distracted. Something for me to fight for and remind myself I'm still alive.

My teeth chatter, my whole body shaking as I submerge deeper in the deep water, trying to imagine the life I had before my parents died.

Nothing comes to mind. No good memories. No happiness. Nothing. All that sits in the back of my mind is pain, suffering, and death.

Lying here in the ice water, I open my eyes and stare up at the emptiness that surrounds me. I'm completely numb in this moment, and I have no urge to *feel* anytime soon.

So I just stay here, shivering in the dark, not breathing.

I don't come up for air until my lungs feel as if they're on the verge of exploding and I know I have no other option but to breathe.

Sitting up, I lean over the bathtub and take in quick, deep breaths, every part of my body hurting as I fight to gain control.

Once I'm able to breathe without my lungs burning, I stand up and step out of the tub, making my way through the darkness to my room.

The warm temperature of the house has my body feeling as if it's on fire as I stare at my reflection in the mirror, taking in the damaged sight in front of me.

Slowly my hands run over the scars on my chest and abs, left there from six years ago. My numbness quickly turns into rage and hatred, taking me over until I'm grabbing for anything within my reach and shattering the mirror with it, until there's nothing left to look at.

Nothing there to show me how fucked up I truly am.

It's the first time in a long time that the blood covering my hands has been my own. Yet I still don't feel shit.

Taking slow, deep breaths, I wipe my cut-up hand off and throw on a pair of jeans and a white thermal shirt before heading out the back door, not bothering to inform my brothers that I'm leaving. Maybe they heard the glass shattering, but if they did they give no indication, don't come running to see what's wrong. They must be preoccupied which is perfect.

There's somewhere I want to go right now.

Somewhere I've been fighting to stay away from since last night, and I need to get out of this damn place before I lose it.

Walking fast, almost running as I leave my house behind, putting distance between my brothers and me I pull out a cigarette and turn down the alley that's a mile away from our property. I look straight ahead as I make my way toward my destination.

I make it ten blocks before I hear someone come up behind me. It's clear they want me to know they're following me, which means this dumb ass believes he has power over me.

The asshole follows me for two blocks, not speaking until he realizes I'm not attempting to run from him.

"What do you have in your back pocket, asshole? Show me. Now."

I keep walking just to piss him off.

"What the fuck is that bulge? I could use a new toy."

A small smirk takes over as I stop and toss my cigarette at the ground, ready to take on whatever this dick thinks he's going to do to me.

"I asked you a fucking question." The voice is closer now, almost right behind me. "Empty out your pocket. I want it, asshole. That and anything worth a shit."

Cracking my neck, I pull the lock from my pocket and slowly turn around, my gaze settling on a tall guy wearing clothes five times too big for his ass.

He gets ready to come at me, but recognition registers in his eyes when he sees the family symbol tattooed across my neck.

"Whoa, my bad. Didn't realize you were one of Locke brothers." He backs away, keeping his hands up so I can see them. "I don't want any trouble, man. My mistake. I'll just be on my way."

Usually I wouldn't let an asshole like that leave, knowing what he's out here doing, but tonight is different. My mind is set on where I want to be, and nothing can change that.

He lucked out, but I have no doubt I'll run into him again out here on the streets. He'll get what's owed to him.

Before I know it, I'm standing on the same street I was last night, looking over at the same small white house that had me distracted from my job.

My jaw flexes as I stand here and stare at the lit-up bedroom at the side of the house.

It was about this time yesterday that she got back from a run or whatever it was she was doing out on the streets so late.

If I timed it correctly, she should be coming down the street right about . . .

My attention gets pulled to the sidewalk when I hear the pounding of her feet hitting the pavement.

A strong urge to go to her hits me the moment her eyes land on me and she stops running.

It's almost as if she's luring me in with the way she looks me over, never turning her eyes from me as she unlocks her front door and opens it.

My heart races in my chest when she slowly shuts the door, her eyes staying on mine until she's out of sight.

It's when I see the curtain in her room move that I hear her bedroom window opening, letting me know I was right.

She's just as curious about me as I am about her.

Maybe I'll feed her curiosity and give her a small taste of the youngest Locke.

I'm pretty sure this will be the last time she leaves her bedroom window unlocked and opened for me.

Kadence

I DON'T KNOW WHAT'S COME over me, asking this dangerous man, this stranger into my room. Even resorting to having him sneak through the bedroom window like a thief in the night, like I'm some teenager hiding him from my parents.

God, if my roommate finds out I have a Locke brother in the house, let alone my bedroom, she'll shit.

She's warned me, and I take that seriously, but the truth is ever since I saw him across the street the other night, he's all I've been able to think about.

Taking a deep breath, I step back and keep my gaze on the window, my heart speeding up when I hear rustling right outside.

He's not even in the house yet, and I'm already going crazy

with anticipation of what's to come.

He pushes the curtain aside, braces a hand on the windowsill, and before I can warn him, remembering the jagged piece of metal sticking out from the frame, he's hoisting himself up and inside.

"Motherfucker," he says loud enough I know my roommate could have heard. The last thing I need is her in here acting crazy.

"Shit, I totally forgot about that," I say and find myself moving a step closer. It's as if I want to help him, like I can't stand to see him hurt. Of course, I know he's dangerous. That much is a fact, but I can't help myself.

He holds his hand out, and I see he has a nasty cut, blood welling up. "Let me grab a wet rag. Hold on."

It's an excuse as much as it is me wanting to see if Melissa has heard. Her door is shut, the light off.

I listen for just a second longer, making sure she's not getting up, then walk over to the sink, grab a clean rag, and run it under the water. We don't have a first-aid kit, not that I know of anyway, so I grab some paper towels, a roll of masking tape, and head back into my room.

I shut the door silently, staring at him, his focus on all my shit scattered around the room.

He starts running his uninjured hand over my stuff as if memorizing it, taking in the feel, the shape of everything. This is grossly intimate in a way, like he isn't just touching my things . . . but me.

But I don't say anything and instead stand here for a moment, letting him get to know me through those artifacts, as if he has every right to even be in here, sharing the same air as me.

"I'm gonna bleed all over your fucking floor," he says softly, his voice deep, serrated, like this knife moving over me, barely touching me but promising to break the skin and draw blood.

"Sorry," I say and walk over to him, handing the wet rag to

him first.

He eyes me like he's surprised I'm willing to help him. Maybe he's not used to anyone not running from him. He doesn't say anything though, and instead takes the rag and cleans his hand off, and his arm where the blood has started dripping down the length. He tosses the rag into the small trash can by my bed.

"Here," I say and hand him the paper towel and masking tape.

"I'm good."

I look at his hand. It's already started to bleed again. Taking matters into my own hands, I grab his arm, wrap the paper towel around his cut, and tape it up.

When I look at him, it's to see him staring at me, this weird, almost frightening expression on his face. It's like this cold rush of air has moved over me, covering me in its icy touch, trying to suck the air from my very lungs.

And he's made me feel this way with just a look.

"Like you said, you'll bleed all over my fucking floor." The words just spill out.

I move a step back on instinct and take in the sight of him. Even now I have no idea why I've brought him into my room, invited the very devil himself into my life.

Yes you do. All it took was a look across the street for you to feel something. He made you feel like you're walking on this razor's edge, about to fall over, drop into the very bowels of hell itself.

His body is lean but muscular and hard. So damn sexy and tempting.

The air is thick, charged, alive. I feel the hair on my arms stand on end, as if they know the man in front of me is dangerous, someone I should get far away from.

With my body still damp from running, my clothes sticking to me, a part of me wants to go back out there and have my feet on the pavement. Running lets me be free, lets me feel alive. It's the only time I feel like I can be by myself, my thoughts my own. Maybe that's how he feels when he's out doing what he does with his brothers.

I swallow, my throat tight, my mouth dry as his eyes stay on me. I don't know what to say. When I opened the bedroom window, it had been this automatic move.

My hands are twitchy, my mind replaying seeing him the other night, knowing he watched me, thinking about what he could do to me if he wanted to.

Dangerous, violent, no fucks given . . . all those things and more have come up in the rumors. The Locke brothers keep to themselves because they don't do social hour. Yet here I was inviting one into my bedroom.

When it comes to Aston Locke, I'm flirting with danger, playing with fire right in the palm of my hand.

"You saw me last night," he growls, moving an inch closer to me. I find myself moving one back. We do this silent dance of me retreating because I know he's a predator and I am the prey.

"Yeah," I finally whisper, my voice soft, distant. I have no doubt he can see how scared I am, smell it on me. It isn't that I think he'll hurt me, which is foolish. This man could do that and I wouldn't be able to stop him. Hell, I invited him into my room like a crazy person.

"You see what we did to those motherfuckers across the street?"

I watch his sexy mouth as he speaks, then lift my gaze to his eyes. God, they are so blue. I don't know what it is about him, but I can tell the youngest Locke has seen some shit, lived through hell itself.

And when I retreat one more step, the door stops me. He places his tattoo-covered hands on the cheap wood beside my head, leans down, and I hold my breath.

"You know who I am?" he whispers against my lips, causing me to lose my breath for a quick second.

I can see in the way he appraises me that he knows who I am from last night. I have no doubt about that. "Yes."

He grins, but it's sadistic in nature, pleased that he made me admit it.

"You're about to learn who I really am soon enough."

Aston

I'M CROWDING HER. SHE'S NERVOUS because of it, maybe even second-guessing letting me into her room.

I inhale. Fuck, she smells good, really damn good.

"I'm Aston Locke, a mean motherfucker that you just let all up in your space." I lower my gaze to her throat, see her swallow, watch the slight curve move up and down. "Tell me your name," I demand with a growl.

I could have said it a little nicer, tried to pretend and be sweet, gentle. But to hell with it; I'm not going to pretend to be someone I'm not.

"Kadence." Her voice is soft and so damn innocent. "Kadence King."

Kadence King.

God, how I want to defile her, make her see what all the hype is about concerning my brothers and me and how rough we are. I can imagine her naked, spread out for me, willing to do whatever the fuck I say. And she would submit to me, let me leave my marks on her, pretty purple and blue fingerprints that showed my ownership.

"What have you heard about the Lockes?" I want to hear her speak, want to know what she knows. Hell, I want to be pressed right up against her, her small body so soft where mine is hard.

I want to breathe the same air as her.

I want to fucking own her.

What the hell?

She swallows again, her breathing hard, fast.

She's nervous.

I lower my gaze to her chest, see the way her tits press against the stretchy material of her shirt. Her nipples are hard, and my fingers itch to touch them.

I might be a dangerous bastard, a violent fucker, but I don't touch a girl without her wanting me to. I'll wait until Kadence begs me, asks me to push my dick deep inside her, making her mine.

"I heard you guys aren't to be messed with." Her voice is low, really damn low. "I heard you keep to yourself, aren't social, and if someone crosses you guys . . ." She trails off, and I lift my brow, wanting more. "That you take care of it in the only way you know how."

"The only way we know how?"

She nods and licks her lips. "With guns and bats, hammers, or whatever else you can find to make it bloody."

I chuckle low. *That's about right.*

"And you thought it was a good idea to let one of us in your room, this close to you?"

She shrugs, and I see something shift over her face. She's trying to be strong.

Cute.

"Maybe not, but too late now."

I grin again. Yeah, it's too fucking late now.

There's something about her, something that grabs hold and won't let go. I don't want it to. I want to suffocate from it, need her to as well. I want her to feel the intensity, crave it, become addicted.

Would she really be scared knowing the depth, the lengths I go with my brothers to make any fucker who crosses us pay? Does she really understand exactly what I'd do to anyone that even so much as breathes wrong in my direction?

No, I don't think she really understands.

For her own good I should walk away, leave her alone so she doesn't have to deal with my shit.

But I'm not.

"Do you want to know more about me?" I stare into her green eyes. She's expressive but also cautious. I wait a heartbeat for her answer, already knowing what she'll say.

"Yeah."

God, that's really fucking good.

"You'll know more about me soon enough." I grin and lean in just an inch, so close our lips are almost touching. It takes a hell of a lot of self-control not to just kiss her, take her, knowing she'd love it. "Until then."

I turn and leave her there shaking, going out the window and feeling more juiced up than I ever have before.

Aston

L EANING MY HEAD BACK, I close my eyes and press my hands against the shower wall as the water beats against my sore muscles, relaxing me just a small bit after tonight's shit storm.

Truthfully, nothing ever fully relaxes me. Nothing has for a long fucking time now.

This lifestyle keeps me tense as hell, ready to take on whatever the fuck is thrown at me. But when you've seen what I have—lived through what I have—on edge is the only way to survive.

I'm doing everything I can not to take that next step that sends me falling into complete blackness that'll swallow me up whole.

Hurting motherfuckers who have hurt others has been my

only way of doing that so far. My only way of feeling just a little bit alive.

Swallowing, I run my hands through my wet hair, my mind trailing back to last night when my body was so fucking close to Kadence's.

Fuck, how I wanted to feel her under my fingertips. How I wanted to taste every inch of her fucking body, leaving my mark on her.

I wanted to own her, make her scream my damn name as if she needs me inside her to survive.

The only problem with that is that I'm dark as shit. I need to know for sure she's ready to let me into her light.

There's nothing gentle about me. Not the way I talk. Not the way I handle others, and definitely not the way I fuck.

I feel myself becoming hard. I imagine my hand wrapped tightly around her sexy little throat as I bury myself deep between those slender thighs of hers, making her scream my name until it hurts.

Her roommate would definitely hear, and probably even the neighbors.

"Mmm . . . fuck," I growl while taking my length in my hand and stroking it to thoughts of her.

I don't remember the last time I've wanted a woman as badly as I want her right now. One look across the street two nights ago, and I knew right away I needed to touch her. To feel her shake beneath me as she comes undone.

I've still yet to do that.

I bite down on my lip, moaning as my strokes become fast and hard, bringing me close to losing my shit.

Fuck, I bet her pussy is nice and tight for me. It'd be a struggle to fit my thickness inside her, but I crave the challenge like I crave the darkness.

With just a few more strokes I feel my balls tighten. I release my load down the shower drain, gripping the wall with one hand as I slowly come down from my temporary high.

This isn't enough for me, imagining being inside her. I want more. I need more.

Stepping out of the shower, I quickly dry off and slip my jeans over my naked body before throwing on an old shirt and reaching for my leather jacket.

I barely make it to the top of the basement stairs before Sterling calls out my name, asking me to meet them in the living room.

"You going to tell us what the fuck happened to your hand last night?" He nods down at my wound that's still bandaged up, the dressing soaked from the shower. I could tell he wanted to ask me about it all night, but I knew he'd wait until our job was done first. "And why the hell you didn't answer your phone when we called ten motherfucking times."

"I cut it on the mirror downstairs." It's not a lie. It's just not the full truth. "Then I went for a damn walk to clear my head. I needed to be alone."

Ever since my parents were murdered and I walked in at the end, getting stabbed three times and left for dead, you can say my brothers have been overprotective.

If it weren't for them, I'd be dead and those murderous motherfuckers who took our parents' lives would be alive, roaming the streets, looking for some other drug addicts to take from.

My parents weren't good. They were fucked in the head. Consumed by their habits. The Locke family name is tainted as shit, and my brothers and I are the only ones left other than my uncle, Killian.

My brothers don't realize, though, that I can take care of my damn self now. I'm not that helpless fifteen-year-old that couldn't defend himself anymore. I've been through hell and back many times that they don't know of.

And I've walked out, unscathed every single time, except that one.

"Don't make me remind your ass what happened to our parents," Sterling says over his whiskey glass. "Everyone in this town paints us as the bad guys, the ones to be feared, but we know more than anyone there's fucks out there a lot more dangerous and twisted than us, little brother." His jaw flexes as he tilts back his glass, emptying it. "We've witnessed it."

"Don't worry." I slip my jacket on and pet King's head as he comes to sit at my feet. He's one of the most loyal pit bulls you'll ever meet. He's a mean fucker, you better believe that, but only when we tell him to be. "I'm always prepared."

"Good." Ace nods down at his hammer, sitting next to his feet. "I'm ready to play anytime."

I smirk and head for the door. "Because you're the most twisted Locke of us all."

As soon as the cool night air hits my face, I place a cigarette between my lips and light it, leaning my head back as I inhale.

It's a little earlier than last night, but I have a feeling I know where to find her.

Exhaling, I make my way toward the trails close to Kadence's house.

There's not one person brave enough in this town to run those trails at night, but I have a feeling Kadence isn't as fragile as she looks.

She obviously can't be that scared if she let a damn Locke into her room in the middle of the night.

Before long I find myself standing off in the darkness, watching

Kadence from afar as she slowly jogs between the trees, stopping occasionally to catch her breath.

She seems unaware of anything around her, making me nervous that she chooses to run these paths alone, so late at night.

What if it wasn't a Locke brother lurking in the night, watching her? What if someone far more dark and twisted than me decides they want her just as badly as I do?

Then what?

I'll be around to find out what. That I'm making sure of now.

Kadence

B EING OUT HERE, ALONE, IN the middle of the
night, feels freeing after being stuck in a stuffy coffee shop,
taking orders all day.

The cool air hitting my face calms me, making me feel alive
as I take these trails each night, knowing I'm the only one around
for miles.

At least so far.

In the two months I've been running at night, I haven't once
seen anyone else out here. It's as if everyone's afraid to come out
after dark in this little town.

As if everyone expects the Locke brothers to be lurking around
every corner, ready to get their hands bloody.

Even though I've heard the stories of how dangerous they are, a part of me has always been curious about the brothers, wanting to know why they are that way.

What drives them into the darkness they seem to survive in.

When the youngest Locke, Aston, looked at me from across the street for the second night in a row, I was quick to let him in, wanting a chance to get to know about him.

It was as if my body had a mind of its own, going right for the one thing that was keeping us apart.

Having him in my room, so close, his breath against my lips, had me going crazy inside.

My heart has never beat so damn fast in my life. Not even during my nightly runs, and if I have to be honest, I haven't stopped thinking about him since.

There's no denying I hope he comes back.

The sound of leaves crunching behind me has me stopping and turning around to see if someone's following me.

My heart is racing like crazy as my gaze scans the darkness around me.

I don't see anyone, so I take off running again, going faster this time.

Of course, the moment I begin to think I'm always out here alone, some crazy person might just pop out of nowhere, proving my ass wrong.

I run for a good three minutes before I hear someone come up behind me, right before I'm yanked back by a hand grabbing my mouth.

I scream, but it's muffled, his hand covering my mouth and nearly my nose.

My lungs start burning, the need to suck in a breath strong, making me fight for survival. I lash out, swinging my arms around, trying to hit him, hurt him.

I make contact with his face, my nails digging into his skin.

He grunts, and the pleasure fills me. I got the fucker. Good. But still he drags me back, farther into the darkness, away from the pseudo-protection of the park lights.

I know if I don't stop this, he'll rape me, hurt me. He'll make me his victim, and that I won't stand for. I won't allow him to dig into my soul, crushing me, making me afraid for the rest of my life.

"You stupid fucking cunt," he grits out. His voice is deep, but it sounds fake, like he's trying too hard to disguise it.

He's a coward.

Before I know what's going on, he has me pushed up against a tree. The side of my face connects with the bark, scraping the skin, causing a burn and pain to take root.

I try to turn around, to fight, even if he is stronger. But he has a forearm on my back, pressing me harder against the trunk, making me stationary for the violence he is about to deliver.

I scream, knowing it won't do a hell of a lot of good. It's late, and that's one of the reasons I come out here. I want to be alone with my thoughts, but it's clear that was a foolish mistake.

"I'm going to make you pay for that."

I know he's talking about the scrape across his face. Good, I hope it bleeds, hope it leaves a mark forever.

Then I hear his zipper being pulled down, and my survival mode kicks in. I fight harder, trying to be strong.

Then, out of nowhere, the weight on my back is gone, and there's a grunt behind me, a sound of flesh hitting flesh. I should run, leave, but my morbid curiosity has me turning and watching the scene unfold before me.

Relief rushes through me, my heart rate slowing down a bit when my eyes lock on *him*.

Aston is beating the shit out of my attacker, and as much as I should feel disgusted by the act of violence, all I can do is watch in awe.

Aston

ALL I CAN FEEL IS my fist going into this motherfucker's face. Over and over I slam my knuckles into this bastard's body, hearing him grunt in pain, smelling his blood coat the air.

The metallic scent that fills my nose tingles, and makes me hungry for more violence.

This prick thought he could touch Kadence. He's about to learn the hard truth that she's mine, and anyone who fucks with her deals with me.

"God."

I hear her whisper, but I'm in my own world, the need to cause more pain, give more violence, rushing through my veins.

My heart is pumping wildly, my head exploding with the power, strength, with the degrading things I still want to do.

"You think you can fucking touch her, hurt her?" I say and pound my fist into his face again. We're on the ground now, me straddling him, wailing on his ass. "You fucked with the wrong girl, asshole." Blood coats my knuckles, splattered on my shirt, but I don't stop.

I can't.

"Enough," she says softly.

But I'm in my own world, wanting to hurt this fucker as badly as I can.

"You'll kill him," she says again, and when I feel her hand on my shoulder, I make myself slow. I look at her, the shocked expression on her face piercing me deep.

I'm breathing hard, my chest rising and falling, blood covering my hands, sweat coating my body. I stand, look down, and see the bastard still breathing. I would have much preferred to kill him, making him suffer.

"He's not worth it," she whispers.

She's wrong about that, but I find myself turning toward her, wanting to touch her, make sure she's okay.

I take a step closer, and she moves one back. We do this several times until she is pressed to a tree trunk, her chest now rising fast and hard.

"He's not worth it," she says again.

I shake my head. "He deserves to be six feet under the fucking ground for even thinking he can mess with you."

I may have stopped, but I have no intention of letting this fucker pass. If she doesn't want to see me take vengeance, fine. But I'll find this prick later, and then real damage will be done.

I lift my bloodied hand up, smooth a finger along her cheek, and stare at the smear of red on her flesh. I need her right now, want to combat this violence running in me with the feeling of her under me.

She's shaking, her breath moving in and out of her parted lips fast. Fuck, I can't help myself, don't even want to at this point.

I wrap my hand around her neck, the hold loose, but letting her know I'm serious. I stare into her eyes for long seconds, seeing her pupils dilate, seeing she is equal parts aroused and frightened.

I'm a bastard, wanting her after what almost went down. But I can't help myself.

Feeling the need claim me, I kiss her, just slam my mouth down on hers and take her lips like I own her.

I do fucking own her. She's mine.

I tighten my hand on her throat, press my body to hers, and feel my dick get hard. Fuck, I want her right now, want to part her thighs and slide my cock into her tight little pussy.

I bet she's tighter than a fucking fist wrapped around my cock. Once I have her, I know she'll be wet for me too, so damn juicy my dick will be soaked, the sheets damp beneath her.

I groan against her mouth, sliding my tongue deeper between her lips, making her take it all, knowing she loves it.

But she breaks away, panting, her lips red, swollen. We stare at each other for long seconds, and finally I take a step back.

"Come on," she's the one to say, and I let her take my hand.

I know where we are going. Tonight I'll show her exactly how much I want her.

Tonight she'll see that she *is* mine.

Aston

THE ROOM IS FILLED WITH silence. Kadence is moving around slowly to clean my hands, as if she's worried her roommate will wake up and find me here.

She can be quiet all she wants while she works on my busted-up hands, taking care of me, but there's no way she'll be able to be quiet once I take care of her and make her mine.

I'm going to make her scream so loud I'll feel it in my fucking soul, overpowering all the darkness around me, allowing me to get lost in *her* for a short time and forget about this hell.

"Thank you for doing that." She lifts her green eyes up to meet mine, her lips slightly curving into a thankful smile as she wraps the last of the bandage around my hand. "There's no doubt he would've hurt me badly if you hadn't been out there tonight. I'm glad you were there, Aston."

Tightly clenching my jaw, I stand over her small frame, allowing her to take me in. She gazes up and down my sweaty body as if she wants to reach out and run her fingers over every dip and curve.

Anger is still swarming through me at the thought that that piece of shit believed he had the right to hurt her and take her without permission.

Fuck that shit.

I'll rip that fucker's throat out before he ever has the chance of that happening.

I can hear her breathing pick up, see the fast rise and fall of her chest as I back her to the door and brush my lips against her smooth neck. "No motherfucker will ever touch you without your permission," I growl. "Not as long as I'm around."

But what I don't say, at least not just yet, is that the only motherfucker who will ever touch her is me.

She lets out a small breath of air as I move my mouth around to the front of her neck then brush up to her lips. "You want me to touch you? You want my hands all over this tight little body of yours, Kadence?"

I hear her swallow before she lets out a quiet, "Yes," across my lips, confirming what I already knew from the first moment our eyes met.

As soon as the word leaves her mouth, my hands are gripping her waist and flipping her around to press her front against the door.

Before she has a moment to catch her breath, I quickly rip her pants down her legs and slam my body against hers from behind, letting her feel my roughness.

A small, needy moan escapes her pretty little lips once she feels my hardness pressed against her ass, ready to take her.

Pressing her harder into the door with my hips, I lift her shirt over her arms before pinning them to the door and grazing my teeth over her throbbing neck, tasting her sweaty flesh. The salt on my tongue has my cock jerking.

"Nothing is gentle about me," I grit out. "You're about to find out just how fucking *hard* I am."

"God, yes."

That's all I need to hear.

Reaching between our bodies, I quickly undo my jeans and slide them down my hips before yanking her panties down her thighs and thrusting into her tight little pussy, fast and deep.

I do it so fucking hard that she turns her head and bites into my arm, almost drawing blood, to keep from screaming.

Groaning against the back of her neck, I wrap my fingers into her thick hair and pull as my other hand reaches around to grip the front of her neck and squeeze.

My thick cock fills her completely, easily sliding in and out from her wetness coating me, our sweaty bodies slapping together with force.

She's so much wetter than I imagined she'd be for me. I can feel her arousal dripping down to my balls.

Fuck, she likes my roughness . . .

This has me fucking her harder, being so rough that her body moves up the wooden door, her face smashing against the surface with each thrust.

"Aston," she pants while gripping at anything she can grab on to. "Keep going . . . don't stop."

I yank her hair back and smirk before running my tongue over her hot neck, all the way over to her ear. "I don't plan to."

Pulling out of her, I flip her around and crush my lips against hers, tugging and pulling with my teeth until her lips are red and swollen. "Not for a long fucking time."

A surprised breath escapes her lips as I pick her up and roughly toss her onto her bed before walking over to stand at the foot of it.

She's breathing heavily, gripping at the blankets as I grab the bottom of my shirt and rip it off over my head, tossing it aside.

I see the expression on her face change the second her gaze scans my chest and abs, taking in the long, jagged scars.

Her focus stays there, examining them, but she doesn't say anything as I lower my jeans, stepping out of them.

I stand here in silence for a moment, my chest quickly rising and falling as she takes in the sight of me, naked, in front of her.

There's no mistaking she's completely turned on by what she sees, but also scared and concerned about what happened to me in the past.

If she knew half the shit I've been through, the suffering and pain I've endured, there's no doubt in my mind that she'd run and never fucking look back.

Now it's time for her to really *feel* me.

Kadence

I STARE AT ASTON, MY pussy sensitive from when he shoved all those hard inches into me, but my body still wants more.

I crave more.

I look at the inked-up skin he reveals, the scars I can see intersecting the art. What must he have gone through? What fucking horrors did he see to make him broken on the outside?

Sure, physically he's strong, powerful, but those scars had to have given him a lasting effect. They had to have chipped away at him.

I want to ask him about them, to comfort him, but a part of me knows better than to pry. I don't want to push it, don't want to cross that line.

Maybe, given time, I'll open up and find the courage to ask him, to let him know I want to make sure he's okay.

But I can see right now talking is not in the plan. It's clear in his eyes that he wants to fuck me, and do it hard.

"Take off the bra. Now," he demands.

I rise up slightly, remove my bra, and once naked I rest on the bed again. He looks me up and down as if he's doing it to get his fill. Goose bumps pop out along my flesh, and I feel myself getting wetter.

"How primed are you for me?"

I don't answer, just brace my feet on the bed and spread my thighs wide, showing him I'm ready for him to take me, to claim me.

He makes this deep rumble in his chest and grabs his huge, thick cock and starts stroking himself. God, the sight of him jerking off while he looks at me is so damn hot I can barely handle it.

And then he's on me, pushing my legs wider apart, settling between them. He doesn't wait to shove back into my body, stretching me, making the pain and pleasure rise to this burn, this high.

The grunt he gives when he's to the hilt inside me, his balls pressed to my ass, has me gasping. I arch my back, thrust my breasts out, and ride the wave of pleasure as he starts fucking me.

In and out. Faster, harder, no fucks given.

He has his hand on my throat, cutting off my breathing slightly, making the intensity wash through my body.

I feel myself go higher, the root of his cock stroking my clit, the weight of his hand on my neck getting me off.

And then he's gently biting my shoulder, soft at first, but with more force the faster his thrusts become. Just when I think I'm going to climax, he pulls out, flips me over, and smacks my ass.

At this point I don't care if Melissa can hear me.

He spanks me hard, the blood rushing to the surface, no doubt my skin becoming ruby red. And then he's pushing my thighs apart, thrusting back into me, and fucking me like a madman.

I grab the sheets, curl my hands around the material, and let myself feel it all.

God, he's so big, so fierce. He thrusts in and out, hard and fast, hitting this deep part of me that has my toes curling and my body feeling as if it's on fire.

Grunting, he presses his hand on the center of my back, making me take all of him.

I feel myself going higher, know I'm going to come. Then it hits me almost like a distant memory, like a dream. He isn't wearing a condom. But in this moment I can't even find it in myself to care.

The youngest Locke brother is inside of me, proving just how fucking rough and raw he is, and it feels too damn good.

"Come on, baby, fucking come for me. I want to fucking hear it." He thrusts deep inside me. "Let me feel this tight little cunt clenching around me, sucking at my cock, needing that cum."

His hand on my back hurts, but it also feels incredible.

And just like that, because he demands I let go, I get off, my body shaking as I dig my nails into his arm, most likely drawing blood.

This doesn't make him stop though.

He pumps harder and faster, his balls slapping my clit, his dominance making me wetter, needier with each thrust.

"That's it. Fuck." He gives my ass a hard smack. "This is only the fucking beginning. You're mine. Only mine."

He buries his cock in me, and I know he's coming. I can feel him filling me up, sense it slipping out from where we are connected.

My thighs are sticky with his cum, the sheet damp below me. I know I'll have bruises come morning, bite marks to prove he claimed me.

And all I can think is that I want more.

I *need* more.

Aston

FUCK, HOW I LOVE WATCHING my cum drip from her tight little pussy and cover the bed below her, showing her she's mine.

Nothing has ever even come close to feeling this damn good, making me feel *alive*. And I know the moment I leave here, that all I will feel is the emptiness that swallows me whole.

But that's what I'm used to. That dark, empty feeling that consumes me.

It's how I live, how I survive.

It's how I stay alive . . . feel alive.

It's not something that can be changed so damn easily, no matter how fucking badly I wish it was so.

Standing from the bed, I look down at Kadence's naked, flushed body. I watch the rapid rise and fall of her chest as she looks up at me while fighting to catch her breath.

Her legs are still spread for me, her sweaty body on display for my viewing as if she's letting me know she's mine.

The cum dripping from between her beautiful legs already confirmed that, and we both know it.

Walking over to the window, I open it and pull out a cigarette, lighting it and inhaling a long drag as the night air hits my naked flesh.

Her gaze roams over my body as I stand here, taking in every hard inch of me as if she can't believe I just took her. It's like she can't believe that I just fucked her so good that the neighbors no doubt heard her cries of pleasure.

No doubt her roommate heard, as well.

I know I should be leaving now. Should be walking out that damn door and hiding in the solitude of my basement, but I don't want to.

Not tonight. Not while her body is covered with my scent . . . my sweat mixed with hers.

Taking one last drag, I snub it on the ledge and toss the cigarette out the window and close it.

I tilt my head when she gets ready to reach for something to clean off with. "Don't."

Locking eyes with her, I crawl back into her bed and roughly pull her body against mine.

Fuck, she smells like me. That has the possessive side rising up in me.

The little moan that escapes her lips is enough to let me know she wants me here just as badly as I want to be here.

"I want me all over your fucking body till morning." I drag

my teeth over her sweaty neck and growl before whispering in her ear. "I want my cum inside you, Kadence. I want you to remember the way I fucked you and claimed you while you sleep."

She doesn't say anything.

She doesn't have to.

Kadence

I WONDER HOW LONG ASTON will stay. I don't want him to go, but I also know that maybe this won't last.

Maybe what I feel isn't what he feels?

He pulls me close, this possessiveness coming from him.

"What happened?" I find myself asking, wanting to know about the scars, wanting to know his truth. I reach out and touch the closest scar to me, one that's across his tight abs.

He pulls away, lying on his back, staring at the ceiling. His jaw is clenched, his focus seeming intense.

"I'm sorry," I whisper, knowing I probably crossed a line.

"It's good." He looks at me. "I don't know if telling you about all this shit is the right thing. I'll scare the shit out of you, if I haven't done so already."

I push myself up, not caring that I'm naked. I don't care about anything but this moment.

He turns and faces me, pulls me in tightly, and I know that no matter what he says, I'm not going anywhere.

I want Aston.

I want to be owned by him completely.

12

Aston

S HIT, SHE WANTS TO KNOW about my scars, about how I got them. I am one cruel motherfucker to anyone who crosses me, but a part of me wants to be . . . gentle with her. A part of me wants to tread lightly. I've never felt like that before. I've never given two fucks about what anyone thought.

If they are stupid enough to ask about us, they get the cold, brutal truth. They find out the hard way who we are.

"My parents were worthless. They were druggies, and we'd have dealers come to the house frequently." I run my hand along one of the stab wounds I got that night. The one across my abs. "My parents pissed a dealer off. It was a deal gone wrong, and he killed them." I exhale, that night flashing through my mind. I stare at her and look into her eyes, wondering what she's thinking right now. "Then the dealer turned that knife on me, meant to kill me."

I have to give her credit; she doesn't look shocked or scared.

"And that's why the Lockes are this way?"

I don't speak for a few seconds, not giving a fuck that my parents are in the ground.

"That's why my brothers are so protective of me. That's why we are so tight with each other and don't let anyone fuck with us."

"Do you miss them?"

How will she feel when I tell her I don't give a shit about my parents? "Our parents were worthless pieces of shit. They deserved what they got and more. Them being dead doesn't even begin to make up for the damage they did to me and my brothers. All the physical and mental hurt they caused us growing up." I feel rage and darkness creep up on me, transforming me, making me feel whole.

I feel its icy fingers stroke my skin, taking hold of my black heart, and squeezing. This is what I live for, and I will never back down from it.

I'll never let it leave me.

If Kadence wants to be in my life, she needs to see every cruel, heartless, and black part of my fucking soul.

"If they were assholes and hurt you and didn't care for you the way they should, good, they deserved what they got."

I'm pretty fucking stunned by her words.

"But I'm sorry you went through that, had to deal with it all."

"It made us stronger." I sit up and start grabbing my clothes. I don't want to go, but I remember I have to go help my brothers.

They'll track my ass down if they have to, and it won't be pretty for anyone.

As much as I want to stay here and fuck Kadence until she can't walk straight, I have to go.

Just as I get the last of my clothes on, there's a knock on the bedroom door.

I see Kadence immediately stiffen.

"Kadence?" the roommate calls out. "Are you okay?"

"Shit," Kadence says under her breath. "I'm good." She goes to get up, gets tangled in the sheets, and falls to the ground, cursing loudly.

"Are you okay?" the roommate says as she opens the bedroom door.

The roommate and I lock gazes, and I watch her terrified eyes grow wide.

I turn and help Kadence off the ground, pull her in close, and kiss her, letting her roommate know she's mine.

I hear the soft moan come from her, and pride fills me. My cock also starts to get hard again.

Damn, I want her.

I pull away from Kadence, sure as fuck not wanting to, but needing to go.

I walk toward the roommate, grinning, not caring that she clearly knows what we just did.

Hell, I'm pretty fucking proud that I claimed my girl.

She moves to the side, allows me to walk by her without any issues. She's afraid, scared as fuck of my reputation, clearly.

I look at Kadence, feeling all kinds of possessiveness slam into me.

My girl.

Then I turn to the roommate again, give a wink, and leave the room.

If Kadence thinks this is the last time I'll see her, she really doesn't understand what it means to be mine.

13

Kadence

MY HEART SINKS THE MOMENT Aston walks out the door. Realization hits me that I have no idea if I'll see him again.

That thought has me feeling sick to my stomach. Worry washes through me, and I wrap the sheet around my body and walk through the living room to watch him out the window as he walks away.

This feeling I have is foreign, strange in the best of ways. I want to see him again, want to feel him on me . . . *in* me.

Melissa standing next to me with her hard, icy glare, making clear how damn angry she is with me, isn't even enough to make me forget about the man who just took me like no other man has before.

The way he handled me and made me feel like I was his and only his has me wanting and needing more of him.

"You have to be insane," Melissa whispers.

Maybe I am, but if feeling this way for Aston makes me crazy, I don't want to be sane.

Aston has me completely wrapped up in him, and I barely even know him yet.

But what I do know . . . is that he's been hurt far worse than he's probably ever hurt someone else before, and I *hate* the thought of him being hurt.

It makes me angry.

"You just had sex with a Locke brother?" Melissa says, pulling my attention away from the empty street. She phrases it like a question, but she knows the truth.

I didn't even get a chance to see him walk away. He must've taken a different route, disappearing between the houses.

"You let one of those dangerous brothers into your bed and into your body? Kadence, what the hell were you thinking?" The panic in her voice is real. She looks me over, standing here naked, still holding the sheet to my body. "He was in our damn house. That's not cool."

"He saved me tonight, Melissa." I let out a breath and walk past her, making my way back to my room. I just want to be alone right now. The last thing I want to do is listen to Melissa put Aston down. "He's not as bad as you think. He makes me feel . . . safe."

"Ha!" She runs her hand over her face and gives me a funny look, showing me again that she thinks I'm crazy.

And maybe I am.

"That's hysterical. A sadistic man makes you feel safe. Did you forget that you just saw him across the street the other night with blood on his hands?"

"Of course not." I place my hand on my bedroom door and look her right in the eyes. "And tonight, there was someone else's blood on his hands. Due to him protecting me. That leaves a bigger impression in my book."

She gets ready to speak but then stops as if she's trying to think of how to respond. "What almost happened? Are you okay?"

My heart speeds up when I feel Aston's cum slowly dripping between my thighs. I'm surprised I'm just now noticing it.

I was so wrapped up in him leaving that I forgot I never went to the bathroom after we had sex.

He wanted me full of his cum, and that thought has excitement moving over me again.

I squeeze my legs shut and answer her. "I'm fine. If it wasn't for Aston showing up when he did, then who knows what would've happened to me. I might not even be here right now."

She gives me a weird look, noticing the way I'm standing. It takes her a few seconds before her eyes go wide as if she's just figured it out. "Oh God. Please tell me his semen is not dripping down your legs right now? He did wear a condom, right?"

My whole body ignites from her question, sending my heart into overdrive. I feel my face heat, the embarrassment of her being so blunt filling me.

I know we should have used protection, but in the heat of the moment all I wanted was to have him inside of me, feeling him between my legs as he claimed me as his.

He's the first man I've let inside of me without protection, but the way he thrust himself into me bare, knowing without question that I'd want it, only seemed to turn me on more in some sick, twisted way.

I know being on the pill can only do so much, but something

tells me he doesn't just randomly sleep around with women. He seemed surprised that I was even willing to let him within breathing distance of me.

The Locke brothers have a reputation that I'm sure doesn't have many women knocking down their door for sex.

My silence has her eyes widening even more.

"Holy shit." She throws her hand over her mouth and takes in the bite marks and redness covering my exposed skin as I stand here smiling at her expression. "Looks like he's just as rough in the bedroom as he is outside of it." She appears curious now and less afraid. "Was the sex at least enjoyable?"

"Honestly . . . I've never come so hard in my life."

I can't believe I told her that, but the words spilled from my mouth and it's the absolute truth. There's no hiding that even if I wanted to.

She stares at me, but I don't feel like justifying myself.

I've never felt this way before, and I don't want it to end. I don't want to pretend that I can let this go, just let Aston go. I've spent too much of my life sticking up for someone that no one else understood, someone that the whole town tore down, little by little until there was nothing left of her to save.

I will not step back now and judge Aston, especially understanding some of what he's been through.

Without knowing what that pained expression behind his ice-blue eyes is all about, I have no right to judge his actions.

Melissa may never understand, and that's because she didn't grow up with my mother. She didn't have kids laughing in her face her whole life because her mother was severely depressed and the talk of the damn town.

All because no one took the chance to ask what my mother had been through.

I will never be one of those people to let others' opinions get in the way and blind me from my own emotions.

Aston Locke is misunderstood.

He's feared by the whole town.

And I want nothing more than to see the real him.

The one that somehow has a way of making me feel safe around him.

14

Aston

I'M SHAKEN AWAKE IN THE middle of the night by one of my asshole brothers pushing me around, not giving a fuck that I'm dead asleep.

I left Kadence's place, not wanting to be without her, but fuck if things hadn't gotten weird with her roommate.

I figure they had shit to talk about since I got caught in her room, and me not being there was probably for the best. Not to mention I had a feeling this would happen and my brothers would've flipped their shit if I was gone.

"Wake your sleeping beauty ass up," Sterling says above me before slapping me across the face to irritate me. "We've got a job to handle."

Pissed off, I wait until he walks away, then I toss a knife at the wall. It skims right past his grinning face and sticks in the old wood.

"Asshole," he mutters, but I hear him chuckle, clearly amused by my angry outburst of violence.

Grunting, I pull my tired ass out of bed and run a hand over my face while exhaling. I glance at the clock. It's still late as hell, but the sun will be rising in a few hours.

Whatever the fuck my brothers want to do will have to be finished while we still have the cover of darkness on our side.

I get ready, head to where my brothers are, and together we leave, ready to take on whatever needs to be handled so damn badly that some fucker is willing to pay us five grand to get the job done.

The atmosphere is pretty fucking somber, and although I don't know exactly what's going down, I know it's a dirty job. They always are.

I let my older brothers handle planning this shit. I just follow along and take care of business. I have been ever since they saved my ass that night.

With grim expressions we climb into the vehicle and head down the road. I pull out my knife and start running my finger over the blade.

It's a habit, one that calms me, one that lets me know I'm in control. I'm the one who holds the fucking power.

We drive for about twenty minutes before pulling into the driveway of an old-as-fuck, falling-apart house.

This is a meet-up spot, no doubt. No one lives here, not unless they are crackheads, or maybe a teenager looking for a spot to get his dick wet.

A few minutes later and another car pulls up beside us, setting my ass on high alert.

You never know what to expect at one of these, so you always need to come prepared.

Once we are all out of the vehicle, we head inside. The stench of mold, age, and decay surround me. I take in the waste, the despair and toxicity.

It's exactly the kind of place a person with a black heart—and one cold motherfucker—would live.

Guess that's why I feel so at home right now.

The guy in front of us looks shifty as fuck. He has two other guys with him, maybe scared being in our presence.

Good, he needs the backup if he decides to fuck us over.

"You can do this?" the guy asks, shifting on his feet, looking around the room, maybe thinking the cops will bust in or some shit.

"Yeah, you want the guy who fucked your sister up real good to get the message," Sterling says, cocking his head to the side. "That's our fucking specialty. But you already know that shit, so don't question it."

"You can't fuck him up yourself?" I'm never one to keep my mouth shut, but then again, all the Locke boys are this way.

We get it from our uncle. There's no doubt about that.

"We don't want our hands dirty in this, and I don't want my sister in danger anymore. If they know it's us, it'll be an all-out war. I just need this prick to walk away from her. I need him to know there's someone out there that has the ability to fuck him up and hurt him worse than he's hurt her."

"It's not a problem," Sterling says and looks at me. I can see in his expression he wants me to shut the fuck up.

Nothing new there.

Hell, it doesn't matter to me, so I shrug. I want this asshole to pay as much as the dick hiring us does.

"You know where to find him?"

Sterling nods. "We got all the information already."

"We'll handle it," Ace adds with a wicked grin.

Yeah, we'd handle it all right. I have some aggression to let out, and a motherfucker who doesn't know how to treat a woman seems like the perfect outlet.

Without another word Ace snatches the envelope from the dude's hand and shoves it in the front of his ripped-up jeans. "Let's go show these motherfuckers who they're dealing with so little brother here can get some damn beauty rest."

"Fuck you," I say with a grin while twirling my knife around. "I'm always down; let's just do this shit."

Really, I just want to get back to Kadence.

My brothers and I pile into the SUV again and head toward the address Sterling was provided with.

I'm surprised as hell to see this asshole lives in the rich part of town. Hell, he probably lives in his parents' basement and gets off on beating his woman, knowing she won't run because he has money and connections to keep her around.

That's some twisted-ass shit.

Sterling slows the vehicle down, creeping in front of the house as we scope it out.

There's no doubt the residents in his neighborhood are nosy as dick and will call the cops the second we step foot out of this thing, looking as rough as we do.

"Well fuck . . ." Sterling punches the steering wheel and turns the SUV around. "We can't do this shit here. That asshole should've known that before he wasted our motherfucking time by sending us to a damn subdivision."

Feeling the frustration and anger beginning to creep in, I pull out a cigarette and take a long drag before slowly exhaling.

It's shit like this that makes me want to go after the idiot that hired us for the job.

I close my eyes and lean my head back on the seat, getting lost in thoughts as we head to the house.

The thought of Kadence instantly gets my cock hard, which considering I'm in the SUV with my brothers, makes me feel awkward as hell. But I don't give a shit when it's all said and done.

What I want to do is get out of the vehicle now, go to her place, and fuck her so she knows that she's mine.

But I'd be an asshole to show up at her house at four in the damn morning, not knowing if she has to be up soon for work.

I have no doubt in my mind I already wore her out for the night. She's going to need as much sleep as she can get to make it through today.

And all the strength she can get for when I claim her again.

Once we pull into the long-as shit driveway leading to the middle of nowhere we call home, my gaze immediately sets on an old Buick parked in the grass.

My brothers must notice it too, because it has Sterling speeding up, now in a hurry to make it to the house.

Whoever the hell is stupid enough to be creeping around our property in the middle of night must not know shit about who we are and what we're capable of.

I'm guessing the asshole never made it inside to break in before we pulled up because King, that big bastard of a dog, would be tearing at the front door right now, ready for a late-night snack.

"I got this fucker." Before Sterling can stop the vehicle, I jump out the back and chase down the stranger who's now running and weaving his way through the trees behind the house.

He has another thing coming if he thinks this little hunt is something he'll get away from unscathed.

Fuck that. Not happening.

The adrenaline pumping through my veins has me catching up with the guy and dragging his ass over to the river.

With force, I throw his body down into the dirt and drag him down to the dirty water. "I guess you don't know what happens to assholes who think they can fuck us over." Growling out, I push his head down into the water and hold it for a few seconds, feeling the darkness consume me as he struggles in my arms.

He sucks in a burst of air the second I yank him up by his hair. "You gonna tell me what the fuck you're doing here, or are you still thirsty?"

"Fuck you," he coughs out. "Not telling you shit."

I tilt my head and smile. "All right, your choice."

Before my words can even register, I have the dick's head back under water, holding it there as I pull out a cigarette and light it, which is harder than hell seeing as the asshole is struggling.

I have all night to do this shit.

"What ya doing, little brother?" Ace walks fast down the hill, grinning like a maniac when he sees the scene before him. "You get more and more like me every day. That shit is scary as fuck. Leave the twisted shit for me. It's all I have left."

Exhaling, I release the back of the guy's hair and give Ace what he wants. We all know he needs this twisted shit to survive more than we do.

"I'll go find Sterling," I say stiffly.

"Don't bother. He found out where the boyfriend was and took off before I could stop him."

I toss down my cigarette and punch the tree, the skin breaking open, the pain lacing up my arm.

"He's alone. Sterling can handle it." He smiles down at the

asshole crawling his way out of the water. "And I'll play with my new friend here."

I have no doubt about that.

These two assholes will be lucky if they survive my brothers tonight.

15

Kadence

THE COFFEE SHOP I WORK at is small, family owned, and older than I am. But I like the owners and feel like I'm part of the family.

They also work with my schedule and allow me to make up my own hours because I take some classes at the community college.

The pay might not be the best, but it allows me to help Melissa with rent and all that shit, and makes me feel like I'm at least contributing.

"Can you clean off the corner table, honey?" Cheryl, the wife of Bryon, and the other owner of this place, calls out from the back room, pulling me from my thoughts.

"Sure," I say, grabbing a rag and heading to the table she's referring to.

All I can think about is Aston, what he's doing right now, if he's thinking of me . . .

God, I am still sore in the best of ways. His passion is unlike anything I've ever experienced, unlike anything I can even think about.

Even my thigh muscles protest as I lean over the table to clean it off. A flash steals over me, the images of what we did last night, of how he fucked me . . . and that's exactly what he did.

Another hour passes, and I clock out, anxious to get out of here. I don't know if I'll see Aston tonight, or again really. He was vague about it all, just up and leaving, making me wonder.

I need a run, need to get this anxious energy out of me. It's still light outside, and I'm not stupid enough to go running at night after what happened.

Once I'm back home, changed into my running gear and my phone shoved into my pocket, I take off. I have no particular place to go, no destination in mind. I just need to run as far and as fast as my feet will take me.

I need to be covered in sweat, my heart racing, the blood pumping through my veins. I need a distraction to keep my mind from being stuck on Aston.

I don't know how long I run, but I end up finding myself at the edge of town, the dirt road that leads to the Locke brothers' house in front of me.

I only know of this place because Melissa made me very aware, when I moved into town, that this is the road I needed to avoid at all cost.

My heart is thundering, and as much as I know I should leave, go back home before it's dark, I still stand here, wanting nothing more than to take the forbidden trail.

It's the sound of tires on gravel that have me glancing over my shoulder to see a dark SUV, the windows tinted, coming right toward me. I move to the side, unable to run back home, knowing this is fucking stupid. Melissa was right; I'm insane.

And when the SUV comes to a stop right beside me, the window rolling down, my heart jumps into my throat.

I know the man in the driver's seat . . . Sterling Locke. The middle brother.

He stares at me, his gaze unwavering, his dark eyes and hair making him seem ominous, dangerous. Hell, he can look like an angel and still be known as the devil himself.

I take note of the tattoos covering his neck, his chest, arms, and hands. But that's not the only thing I notice.

Blood on his knuckles, splattered on his shirt, his skin.

And then he grins at me, this demonic-looking expression that has my blood going cold.

"I've seen you," he says. "Get in." That smile is gone, his voice hard, sharp.

I should go, could probably lose him in the woods. But I'm not that stupid. They live out here alone, away from everyone for a reason.

To think he can't find me, that he probably doesn't know where I live, is fucking dumb to even contemplate.

"I don't hurt women," he finally says. "Besides, I know Aston saw you last night."

This surprises me. Maybe that realization flickers over my face, because he laughs, low, amused.

"If you think my brother and I don't know what the fuck is going on with our youngest, you must not know us very well." He unlocks the passenger-side door. "Get in. Aston is at the house, and I'd like to know what the fuck is really going on with you two."

And I find myself walking over to the door, opening it, and climbing in.

God, did I just accept an invitation into hell?

16

Aston

FUCK. I WISH MY ASSHOLE brother would hurry the hell up and get his ass back home.

All I want to do is go see Kadence, to put my hands on her sexy little body and possess her. I've been itching to since the moment I left her alone, but there's no way I'm leaving this property until I know Sterling is safe, until I know the job is done.

He hasn't been back since he left last night to take care of that douchebag, and apparently his phone is dead because it's been going straight to voice mail since early this morning.

I don't like this shit. Not one bit.

It has Ace's crazy coming out as he paces around the porch with his precious hammer, randomly slamming it into anything within its vicinity.

He's going to bust the whole damn house down soon if Sterling doesn't show his ass.

Hell, I'm even anxious as fuck right now, playing my damn guitar as a distraction, something to keep the demons at bay before I lose it like our eldest brother.

"I'm going to kill that asshole myself," Ace grits out while practice swinging his toy. "Hope he likes the taste of titanium, because if he *does* make it home, I'm knocking his motherfucking teeth out for making us worry."

"It's not the first time he's left us sitting around with our thumbs up our ass," I say stiffly while carefully setting down my vintage guitar. "If it were me out there, you fuckers would be searching the streets for my ass, knocking down doors to find me. Hell, I wouldn't be surprised if your crazy ass burned down every house just to get to me."

Ace swings his hammer around and then leans against the old porch railing, his dark eyes landing on me. "Damn straight. We almost lost your ass once already. You don't know what kind of fear that puts in a man. It makes killing an easy fucking decision, little brother."

Headlights coming down the dirt road have both me and Ace standing tall, anxious to see if it's Sterling pulling up and not another idiot who thinks he can pull one over on us.

King's silence as he watches the vehicle get closer lets us know that it's Sterling and not a stranger approaching. If it was anyone but one of us, King would be barking and ready to attack.

"Lucky bastard." Ace growls and jumps over the railing, walking to stand in front of the vehicle, not giving two shits if he gets run over.

The tinted-out SUV gets within a few inches of hitting Ace

before Sterling stops it and kills the engine.

I stand back with a smirk and watch as Ace swings out, punching Sterling in the face the moment he steps out of the vehicle. "Calm the fuck down, big brother." After wiping his thumb over his bloody lip, Sterling cracks his neck before head butting Ace, sending him stumbling back a bit. "I had a rough damn night, brother. It took longer than I expected. Had to make sure that motherfucker knew to never lay his hands on a woman again." He holds up his bloodied, broken-up fists. "He got the message loud and clear."

Blood covers his shirt and neck, a testament to the violence that he delivered, the violence that runs in all of us.

Everything goes silent, every one of us Locke brothers freezing the moment the passenger-side door opens and Kadence steps out, looking unsure.

I feel King move beside me, but I quickly put my hand out, silently commanding him to stay.

He won't hurt Kadence—hell, he'd hurt us before going after a woman—but I'm doing this for her peace of mind. To let her know she's safe.

Closing the door behind her, Kadence leans against the Expedition and takes her time looking us over before speaking. "Hi." I can tell she's trying to be strong, act brave even. But the tiny signs of her nervousness are clear. "I don't know what I'm doing here. I should leave. I . . . I should go . . ."

"Stay," I command as I watch her chest quickly rise and fall. "Don't fucking move." The sight of her has my damn heart pounding out of my chest, eager to get to her and claim her before one of these assholes get the idea that she's available.

"Well fuck me . . ." Ace says while looking her over with a side smirk. The asshole has charm when it comes to women, with his clean pretty-boy looks, but the dick is the most twisted of us all.

And that's pretty fucking twisted.

Before Kadence can even react to my brother's gaze on her, I'm coming up beside her, pulling her tight little body against me to let my brothers and her know she's *mine.*

This has my brothers smiling, reminding me how much they love a challenge.

Too bad for them, because after the way I *fucked* her hard last night, filling her tight little pussy with my cum, there's no way they're going to touch her.

Or that she's going to want them to.

Kadence is mine in every fucking way, and we both know it.

I just need my brothers to know that shit.

As much as I was wanting to see Kadence tonight, to feel her fucking skin all over mine as I claim her, having her here at the Locke house was the last thing I expected or wanted.

Not this damn soon.

Kadence

EVERY SINGLE ONE OF THE Locke brothers has their eyes on me, taking me all in. I can't hide the fact that it has my legs shaking below me, about ready to give out and send me to my knees before them.

Not from fear but from the raw intensity these brothers possess. They have the ability to bring any girl to their knees with just one look, and to be honest, I can barely handle Aston looking at me that way, let alone all three of them.

Holy hell . . . what have I gotten myself into?

"If one of you motherfuckers so much as breathes on what is mine, I'll cut your little peckers off without batting a damn eye." Aston's harsh tone has his brothers looking surprised.

As if they're not used to him staking his claim on something— or better yet, *someone.*

I look over at Aston, my heart beating wildly in my chest, my palms sweating. I was so nervous when I got in the car with Sterling, and even more so when I got out, not knowing what to expect.

I hope like hell I'm at least playing my calm well enough, so I'm not standing here looking like a terrified little girl in front of the three bad wolves.

Aston has me partially behind him now, his hard body blocking me from his older brothers as he stares them down, standing tall and firm.

The possessiveness is coming from him like a damn wrecking ball, about to tear down any asshole who gets in his way, family or not.

I can't help but feel this thrill rush through me at that.

I'm not exactly sure what's going on, but I have a feeling that trying to exert my independence, maybe making everyone know I can handle myself, can take care of myself, is not the best route to go.

These men are a breed of their own, dangerous and powerful, dominating and territorial.

I need to tread lightly.

"Shit, little brother." Sterling leans against the dark vehicle, looking amused as he takes in Aston's body in front of mine. "It looked like your girl needed a ride, so I gave her one. That's all. I didn't touch her, so calm your dick."

"Well damn," the oldest Locke adds with a twisted grin. "Since when the fuck did you get all possessive over a girl and shit?"

"Since I made one mine," Aston says with a confident smirk. "So back the fuck off. I'm taking her downstairs and away from you horny assholes."

I find myself swallowing as Aston grabs my hand and begins pulling me along with him toward the back of the house.

When you first step inside there's a set of stairs that leads right down to the basement, to where I assume Aston's room is.

The thought of what could possibly happen down here, alone with the youngest Locke, has my whole body buzzing with need, ready to feel him on my fucking skin again.

Aston

I TAKE KADENCE TO MY bedroom, away from the
prying eyes of my fucking brothers.

Although I know they won't mess with her because I
made it clear she's mine, I'm not taking any chances on them eye
fucking her.

"That was . . . intense," she says, her voice soft, her focus on
my room.

It's pretty fucking sparse, only the essentials, but it's one of
the only places I can think if I need my space.

And all I can think about right now is being with her, fucking
the hell out of her, really making my claim known. I want my brothers to hear, to know she's mine, that her screams are for me only.

"I'm sorry," she says. "I needed a run and I somehow ended up . . . here. Your brother saw me and told me to get in the vehicle. I can leave if it makes you uncomfortable."

I hear what she's saying, but she doesn't need to explain herself to me. The fact that she somehow found her way to me only turns me on more, making my need to be inside her grow.

"Come here," I say, my voice deep, my cock hard. She has this little running outfit on, the clothes tight as hell, her tits on display.

Her nipples are hard, and the scent of her clean sweat fills my nose. She'll be even sweatier once I'm done with her.

She comes close to me, her breathing ragged her desire clear.

"How wet are you for me?" I reach behind and grab her hair, yanking her head back until our eyes meet.

I kiss her, making her take my tongue, suck on it, want more of it. I grow harder from Kadence's flavor, the way she feels against me, the fact that she wants this just as badly as I do.

"I'm going to fuck you so hard you can't walk straight tomorrow."

She gasps against my lips, and I kiss her harder, grazing my teeth over her mouth and drawing blood.

"God, Aston."

I turn us around, lay her on the bed, and take a step back, admiring her sexy little body that's meant just for me. "No, not God, but you'll be screaming his name once I'm done with you."

Kadence

I'M SO LOST IN ASTON I can't think straight, can't even breathe. He has our clothes off before I can even contemplate what's happening.

I don't care though because I want this so badly I can taste it.

"Get on your hands and knees," he grits out.

I obey, because it turns me on to do what he says, to know he likes it when I am good and obedient. I can see it in his eyes, in the way his breathing changes.

When I'm in the position he wants, I glance over my shoulder, seeing him grabbing his huge cock, stroking it from root to tip.

"You want this in you, stretching you, making you feel good?"

All I can do is nod. I'm so wet, my thighs damp, my clit tingling. I need him in me, showing me know what it feels like to be possessed, to be owned.

"I want you screaming, want your cries to fill this fucking house." He's on the bed, his hands on my hips, his hard cock right between my legs, so damn close. "If you're going to be in this motherfucking house, I want my brothers to hear you, to know that you're mine."

I'm breathing so hard now, so fast.

I feel him reach between us, place the tip of his dick at my entrance, and in one thrust he's buried in me, making me take all of his huge, thick inches.

I gasp, my eyes watering from the intrusion, from how damn good it feels.

And then he's fucking me, shoving into me and retreating, over and over. I cry out, the feeling of pleasure and pain too much to handle, too much to bear.

His hand reaches around to grip my throat, him squeezing as he buries himself deep, showing me and everyone within hearing distance that I'm his.

It turns me on more than he could ever fucking know.

The sheets are tangled between my fingers, my nails aching

from how hard I dig them into the mattress. I'm going to come and he's just started, just filled me.

And then he grabs hold of my hair with his other hand and yanks my head back hard. I do come them, crying out how good it feels to have him take me. To have Aston all over my fucking skin.

Before my body can come down from its orgasm, Aston has me lifted off the bed and my back slammed against the wall, taking me hard and deep again.

The wall shakes from our weight against it, my body moving up and down the surface as he fucks me hard. So fucking hard that I'm screaming again, no doubt his brothers hearing every last second of my pleasure as the youngest Locke stakes his claim on me.

I can barely breathe, his strong hand tight against my throat, his body pressed so hard against mine. And I love it. I want more of it.

Screaming, I dig my nails into his muscled back, feeling his flesh under my fingernails as he continues to pound his cock into me. Our mouths are so damn close it's like we're both fighting for air.

Leaning in, I bite his lip and tug, causing him to shove inside of me and stop. When he doesn't move for a few seconds, I bite him again, but harder, feeling him smirk against my lips.

"You want more. Good, because I'm not done yet."

With that he tosses me back down onto the mattress and flips me over before slamming into me and cupping my breasts in his hands.

"God, Aston." I yell that repeatedly, not sure if I'm saying it in my head or the words are spilling from my lips.

"Yes, so fucking good," he grunts, smacks my ass in a bruising sting, and makes me get off again. I know there will be a bruise in the morning.

I want it. I crave it.

And when I feel him tense behind me, I know he's getting off, know he's filling me up with his cum. He has a tight hold on my hips, a painful grip.

I want those black and purple fingerprints on my flesh, a mark of his passion, of his need.

I collapse on the bed, not able to breathe, not able to even move. He only fucked me for a short time, but God, I can't even feel my legs.

I guess he got that right.

18

Aston

I DON'T KNOW WHAT THE fuck Kadence was thinking, coming to the Locke house like she did, but damn, I'm glad she's here and in my bed.

I'm glad my brothers now know she's mine, and that I'm not letting her go.

She fell asleep shortly after we had sex for the second time tonight, her body worn out from mine claiming hers.

I'm just hoping like hell my brothers and I don't get a call to take care of a job tonight, because sitting here, playing my guitar softly as she sleeps is the only thing relaxing me and keeping me calm.

I haven't felt this kind of peace in a long fucking time, and I don't want to let it go. With the darkness that was eating me up earlier today, I need this right now.

I need *her* right now.

But I should've known it wouldn't last for long, because her roommate no doubt has no idea where she's at. And she'd freak out knowing that she's here, with me, in this house.

Which is exactly why her phone is now vibrating across the floor.

The sound of her cell has Kadence sitting up quickly looking panicked as she searches for her phone.

She looks good sleepy and well fucked.

"Oh shit!" She scrambles across the bed and bends over me to get to her phone. "Melissa is going to have a heart attack because I'm not home yet."

By the time she goes to answer the phone, it's already stopped ringing.

"Come here," I say while setting my guitar down and pulling her naked body over to straddle my lap. "I'll drive you home if you want." I grip the back of her hair and graze my teeth over her neck. "Or you can sleep in my bed."

She lets out a small gasp as if she's surprised by my offer. I've already claimed her as mine, so you better fucking believe I want her sleeping in my bed.

Just as she gets ready to say something, her phone goes off in her hand again, causing her to lean back and exhale in annoyance. "I should probably go home before Melissa loses it even more and sends out a search party. I hate that she worries." She eyes me. "But then again she probably has good reason to if she thinks I'm with you." She smirks.

Damn right.

Tilting her head to the side, I run my tongue up her neck,

stopping below her ear. "Fuck, I could do this all night with you if we had the time." I grip her ass and pick her up to set her on the ground. "Get dressed. I'll throw on some jeans."

Once I get my jeans on, I reach behind me and slide my pistol into my waistband—a normal thing for us Lockes to do when leaving the house so late at night and by ourselves.

I'm surprised when I feel Kadence slowly run her hand across the handle before her lips come down to gently kiss my shoulder.

"Have you ever had to use this thing?"

I nod my head and clench my jaw at the memories. "I've put a bullet in a few motherfuckers that deserved it, yes. But I haven't killed anyone."

I hear her swallow from behind me. Her breathing picks up as if me having this pistol is a turn on. "You should get me home."

After we're fully dressed, we make it upstairs to the back porch to find my brothers smoking a joint in front of a small fire.

Ace immediately rushes over to stand in front of us while taking a hit. "Well shit. I think our baby brother needs a few hits after all that hard-core fucking downstairs."

"Not now, asshole. Gotta get Kadence home."

"I'll take a few hits." Kadence snatches the joint from Ace's hand, surprising us all.

"She's a keeper," Sterling yells over at us with a laugh. "Hell, she hasn't run off yet. She's braver than most we know."

"I've been through more than you might think. If I learned one thing throughout my childhood, it's that you can't judge others just by what you hear. There's a reason everyone is the way they are." Kadence's gaze meets mine as she takes a hit off the joint and then slowly exhales. "Being scared isn't something I want to do anymore. I refuse to. After losing my mother last year, I fought too hard to be brave just to give up now and wither in a fucking corner."

On instinct my arm wraps around Kadence's waist and I pull her against me as if to protect her from anything she might fear. "And you'll never have to be fucking scared again. I will tear down any fear that ever threatens to haunt you."

I grab the joint from her hand and take a few quick hits before tossing it back to Ace. "I'm driving her home and I'll be right back."

Kadence

I GLANCE OVER AT ASTON, wondering what in the hell I've gotten myself into.

I'm head over heels for this guy, and I don't even know how it happened, but ever since the first night I laid my eyes on him, he's consumed my thoughts.

I don't know why I took those hits when Ace offered me his joint. I'm not even a pot smoker, but I needed something to mellow me out, and it seemed like the perfect time.

The images of what we did in Aston's room play through my head, making my want and need for him grow again. This man has a way of making me crave him, like my darkest desire.

As it is my thighs are sore, the slight stickiness of Aston's cum on the inside of my panties, making me acutely aware that he claimed me.

I shift on the seat and notice he glances at me.

"You okay?"

I nod, my face heating.

"I bet your panties are wet with my cum, aren't they?"

I find myself gasping, the shock of hearing him so blunt still unusual for me.

He smirks, and the sight of the corner of his mouth kicking up has my inner muscles clenching.

That wicked smile always gets me. It's so unbelievably sexy in every way.

God, I can't believe I want him right now again. I am still sore from the other two times we had sex, and that wasn't even that long ago.

"Go on, admit it," he says. "Tell me how wet your panties are from my cum."

My face burns as I grip the seat, needing something to dig my fingers into.

I contemplate lying, but in all honesty I don't want to.

"You know they are wet."

He groans, this deep, rough sound that makes me tingle all over.

Before long we are pulling up to my place, and I'm disappointed our little sex conversation can't go on.

The living room light is on, and I know Melissa is waiting up for me, so sitting out here too long will have her blowing up my phone again.

Before we left his place, I called her, listening to her ranting about how worried she was. But the thing is, I didn't tell her I was with Aston.

Of course I have to. I have to admit that I am with him . . . that I am his.

And as crazy as it is, I look forward to admitting that. I'm not ashamed one bit that Aston has claimed me as his own.

"Good." Aston's voice is deep and full of need as he reaches between my legs and cups me. "Remember that if any fucker tries touching what is mine."

I close my eyes and suck in a breath as he wraps his hands into the back of my hair and leans in to bite my bottom lip. "Fuck, I need you, Kadence. I need us. Tell me you want the same."

"Yes," I admit. "I want this . . . us."

"Fuck . . . I could listen to those words leave your lips all damn night."

My breathing picks up as his tongue swipes across my lips before slipping between them.

I'm not sure I'll ever get used to the sinful taste of Aston's mouth.

Once our lips separate, he releases the grip on my hair to place his hands on my face.

I find myself swallowing as his eyes meet mine and hold my gaze. "I'm sorry about your mother." My eyes close as his thumb gently brushes my cheek, comforting me. "I want to know what you've been through, Kadence. And if you didn't need to get home right now, then I would've stayed up all fucking night learning about your life and everything that hurts you. I'm fighting really fucking hard to let you go right now."

I'm not really sure what to say, so I just nod and offer him a small smile.

I haven't really gotten to see this softer side of Aston yet, and I have a feeling it'll only make me fall for him more.

19

Aston

WE CLIMB OUT OF THE vehicle, and I want to immediately pull Kadence against me again, keeping her as close to me as possible.

I should stay in the car, go home, and let her deal with this. But a part of me wants to protect her, wants to be there for her.

Always.

But there's something in the air, something thick, almost ominous. I look around, not knowing what it is but understanding this sensation, this pull on my skin.

We're not alone. I know this feeling well. It's something I've become used to over the years.

I instantly bring Kadence closer, and I can see she's worried, not sure what the fuck is going on.

"What's wrong?" she asks, her voice raised, her worry clear.

"Shhh, baby." I scan the area, and that's when I notice the guy standing across the street, right in front of the house.

I can't see him clearly, just a dark figure in the shadows, but I know he's one of the fuckers from the other night, the night my brothers and me fucked them up.

He's probably been waiting for his chance to get back at one of us, and this asshole would be smart if he ran inside and told his little friends about me being here alone.

I push Kadence behind me, this protective instinct rising up. The need to protect her is the only thing running through my fucking head right now, consuming me.

Once I see that he's not moving from his spot, I grab Kadence's hand and quickly begin guiding her to the house, needing to get her inside so I can relax a little. "Come on," I demand. "Let's go. Now."

Without question she speeds up in front of me, allowing me to walk behind her, my body protecting hers, all the way to the door. I don't even wait for her to look for her house key before I reach out and turn the knob, hoping like hell that it's unlocked already.

Relief washes through me as the handle turns, allowing me to push it open and get her inside.

"Make sure you lock this door as soon as I walk away. Got it?"

She nods her head and turns the lock. "There. It's already locked . . ."

Before she can finish what she's saying, I grip her face and crush my lips against her, feeling a rush of air leave her lips as I pull away and look her over.

"I'll be out here for a while. Get some sleep."

"Do you really think he's going to try something?" she asks, sounding a bit nervous. "I don't want anyone to hurt you."

My lips turn up into a small smile as I take a step back. It's fucking cute that she's worried about that asshole hurting me. "Don't worry about me, babe. He'd be stupid to try."

Once the door is closed and I see the light turn on in Kadence's bedroom, I head back out to the SUV, lean against the back and pull out a cigarette.

I need something, anything, to calm my nerves right now. Even the slightest idea that Kadence could possibly be in danger has me feeling like a fucking madman, ready to explode at any second.

Placing the cigarette to my lips, I take a long drag and slowly release the smoke as I scan the area once more, to see that motherfucker just standing there, staring, trying to be intimidating.

After the hell I've been through, he's gonna have to try a lot fucking harder than that.

Still . . . it angers me to have him out here and so close to her.

I don't go after him though, not with the bastard just staring, although I want to. I'll leave him be right now, watch him, make sure he doesn't fuck things up or mess with Kadence.

Tossing down my cigarette, I get in my vehicle and watch him. I'll stay out here all damn night if it means I'm going to make sure she's okay.

Hell, I'd prefer to have her at my place, where I know she'll be safe, where I know I can better protect her.

But I also know I can't smother her. She needs to be at her place, needs to feel at home. But I'm not gonna pretend that having this fucker just watching and waiting isn't working my ass up and making me want to kill him.

I'm so focused on the house across the street I don't even realize someone is beside my car until the sound of knocking on my window draws my attention. I turn to see Melissa standing there.

I roll down the window and immediately notice how nervous

she is.

"I'm not going to hurt you," I say. "We don't fucking hurt women."

She glances away, her focus on the ground.

"Yeah, but I know how dangerous you guys are." She lifts her head and looks at me. "Everyone knows."

Well, yeah, that's the truth, but she should have also heard we protect women if it comes down to that.

"I just want to make sure Kadence is in good hands, that this isn't some random hookup for you. I can't just stand back and let my best friend get hurt."

I have to give the girl credit; for being afraid of us, she sure has some balls of steel.

I smile, not trying to be a bastard. "If I wanted her for a piece of ass, I wouldn't be here. I wouldn't still be seeing her after I've already had my cock in her pussy, nor would I have made it known to everyone that she's mine."

Melissa's eyes widen, and I grin wider.

"She's mine." I say it harder, wanting Melissa to know I'm not going anywhere. "Now go inside and lock the door. I don't like you girls being outside when that asshole across the street is. Got it?"

After a second she nods and heads back inside.

I glance across the street again, and see the fucker is gone. But I'm going to hang out for a while, because leaving right now is not something I'm comfortable doing.

If shit is going to go down, I'm going to be here to handle it.

Even if that means sleeping in the damn Expedition.

20

Kadence

The next day

MELISSA HAD AN EARFUL TO give me the second I stepped into the house last night and shut the door behind me.

I understand where she's coming from. I do. We've been friends for as long as I can remember, and we've always had each other's back, no matter what.

Even when all the kids at school made fun of me because of my mother's mental instability, her sometimes not leaving bed for weeks, Melissa was the one who stood up for me and offered to ask her parents for permission for me to stay with them from time to time.

It's not surprising that she's still feeling the need to protect me after all these years.

When my mother decided to take her life last year, Melissa begged me to move closer to her and told me she'd be there for me always.

I hesitated at first, not wanting to leave the safety of my hometown, but after months of my mother being gone, moving in with Melissa seemed like the best thing for me.

Especially with all the judgment and whispers being thrown around behind my back. People believing one day I'll end up like my mother, allowing the whole world to cripple me and hold me down.

That's what my mother did. It started out with my grandparents beating her and abandoning her before she even turned sixteen. My mother met my father shortly after that, and he took care of her.

But after a while he couldn't take it anymore. Couldn't handle her waking up in the middle of the night, crying and popping pills. So . . . he left too.

Left the both of us, and after that everything went to shit, rumors being spread until there was nothing left of my mother, no strength or will to live.

Then one day I found her lying on her bedroom floor, not breathing.

She overdosed, looking for a way to escape. A way to run away from all the rumors and twisted facts about her and her life that people chose to believe because *no one* could understand the suffering she'd been through.

I guess you can say that's why I was drawn to Aston in the first place. I wanted to get to know the real him. To see and *feel* the scars that made him who he is today.

Sighing, I look down at my tea, the liquid swirling around, the steam rising above it.

"You know I just worry because I care about you."

I glance up at Melissa and smile, thankful that she's been such a good friend to me. "I know, and I care about you too, but I really do feel connected with him."

Melissa smiles, her mood toward him seeming different now for some reason. "Yeah, I spoke to him briefly last night when you got in the shower."

That surprises me, and I'm curious about what they said.

"Basically he said I have nothing to worry about because he's claimed you." She scoffs. "Sounds like a caveman."

I start to laugh, picturing what her face must've looked like when he told her this.

"But if you're happy, I'm happy for you."

I let her words play through my head. "I'm happy." I find myself grinning. "He makes me feel like there's something to look forward to. I haven't felt this way in . . . well . . . ever."

"Good, then I'm going to stop worrying so much, or try not to at least." She grabs her bag and stands. "I gotta head to work. Please, just text me or call me this time if you plan to stay out with him late."

I stand and give her a hug. "Sorry, I know. I should've done that, and I will from now on."

"Good. Enjoy the rest of your break and don't work too hard."

I watch her leave the coffee shop and sit back down to finish my break and drink my tea. My thoughts instantly go to Aston, about what he said to Melissa and how he makes me happy.

I want to know more about him, want to have him in my life, bond with him.

I want him to be mine as much as I'm his.

The future is still unknown, but that's part of the appeal, wanting to see where it leads me.

Aston

I PULL MY HARLEY UP at the coffee shop Melissa said Kadence works at, and kill the engine, my mind being made up about being seen in public.

Feeling a bit anxious, I slide my helmet off and jump off my bike, setting it on the seat.

I flex my jaw, feeling gazes on me as I run my hand through my messy hair, smoothing it back while placing a cigarette between my lips and lighting.

It's been a while since I've been out during the daylight, around the prying eyes of this nosy-ass town, judging me. It's something I try to stay away from.

But after spending all of last night and most of this morning sitting outside Kadence's house, I woke up and instantly wanted to go back to her.

This need taking over, wanting to make sure that fucker didn't try anything after I left.

Although Melissa told me Kadence was safe, I couldn't help but want to witness it for myself.

Which is exactly why I'm here, standing in the open, with gazes all over me.

Standing tall, I take a few drags off my cigarette, keeping my focus straight ahead as the whispers surround me, everyone taking this moment to try to figure out what I'm doing in town.

I know they are all afraid of me, of the things I've done with my brothers to exact revenge. But if they don't fuck with me, I won't bother them.

Everything in this damn town is so close together that it's not just the people at the coffee shop getting this very rare glimpse of me, but everyone at the convenient store next door and the hair salon on the other side.

I can still feel their gazes on me, their curiosity making it impossible to turn away as I toss my cigarette down and make my way to the door.

If it was dark out, I guarantee each and every one of these people would be running fast and locking their damn doors, afraid of what I'd do to them.

Smirking, I turn around and give them all a good view of my face before I open the door and step into the coffee shop.

The scent of coffee and baked goods slams into my nose, surrounding me, momentarily making me feel like I've stepped off a damn cliff and entered a different world.

The amount of times I've actually been in a coffee shop, diner, or hell, anywhere that had a group of fucking people in it, equals zero.

And I sure as fuck wanted to keep it that way, but for Kadence I'd do anything.

That realization slams into me, and I falter in my steps. Fuck, she's so embedded in me it's hard to even fucking think straight.

I don't see Kadence right away, so I take a seat at one of the back tables, away from everyone, the shadows partially obscuring me.

And then I see her walking out from the back, her bag over her shoulder, her focus on her phone. God, she's so fucking hot, so mine.

I rise, walk over to her, and in front of everyone pull her close.

She gasps and looks up at me with wide eyes, her surprise clear.

Keeping her body flush against mine, I cup the back of her head, aware everyone is watching us, their scrutiny clear, potent.

I don't give a fuck.

And when I lean in and claim her mouth, press my tongue between her lips, make her taste me, take me, I hear her moan.

"Kiss me back, baby." I pull her in closer, harder. "Let's give these fuckers a show. Let them see you're mine."

I feel her smile against my mouth.

After a long minute I pull back, loving how her mouth is red, glossy, and so fucking lush.

"Let me take you out, show you off." I never do this shit, never wanted to go this route. But with Kadence I want to do a lot of fucking things I never thought I would.

She seems surprised again.

I grin. "Let me wine and dine your sweet ass."

She laughs, and I pull her in for a hug, loving the feel of her against me.

"So, what do you say, baby?"

She makes me wait for an answer, this sexy smile on her beautiful face.

"Yeah, wine and dine my sweet ass. Let the world know I belong to the youngest Locke brother and I don't care what the hell they think."

I grin. That's what I'm talking about.

Kadence

B EING OUT IN PUBLIC, DOING normal every-
day activities is something I know Aston doesn't do very
often. Maybe never. Which makes this moment so damn
special, only making it that much easier to allow myself to fall for
him even deeper than I already have.

I'm lost in this man, and I don't care who knows.

When we walked in the door over thirty minutes ago and
asked for a table, I could see the way people looked at him. I could
see in their eyes how much they feared him.

Could see the judgment.

Didn't matter to him though. All that seemed to matter was
him taking me out and treating me to the night he believes I deserve.

He's barely taken his eyes off me since we sat down, and I love it.

But truthfully I don't need these kinds of things from him. I don't need a nice dinner out in public for him to show me how much he cares.

I realized that the second we walked inside and all I wanted to do was get him alone again.

All I need is for him to touch me the way he does.

For him to kiss me and take me like no other man ever has or ever will.

As much as I love us being here right now, showing everyone that he's mine and I'm his, I want to do something for *him*. I want to show him that I don't need this nor want it.

He's what I want. *We're* what I want.

"Let's get out of here." I toss my napkin on the table and walk over to him, leaning down to wrap my arms around his neck. "Take me to your place. I'd rather be alone with you. There are too many eyes on my man, and I don't feel like sharing you . . . ever."

His lips curve into a small smirk as he stands up and yanks me to him. "You don't want to finish your food first?"

I smile and shake my head. "We'll take it to go and eat it for a late-night snack. I don't have anywhere to be tonight now that Melissa knows I'm yours."

With a small growl he leans in and bites my bottom lip, pulling it into his mouth. Goose bumps cover my flesh as I feel the tip of his tongue swipe across where he just bit me.

He doesn't bother pulling his mouth away from mine as he digs into his pocket with his free hand and tosses some cash onto the table.

"Fuck, baby. I love the sound of that." He possessively grabs my hip and begins walking us to the door. "Let's get the fuck out of here so I can have you to myself. Forget the food. There's plenty at the house."

WE'VE BEEN STRETCHED OUT ON Aston's couch for the last hour, the house empty, his brothers gone. Although I didn't finish my dinner, I'm feeling full, content. As if being here with Aston in the comfort of his arms is all I need.

But what makes me feel even better is the fact that Aston went out of his way earlier, went against his comfort, and took me out. I still haven't stopped thinking about how he did that for me. He may be a hard-ass who thinks he has no heart, that his soul is black, but he's proved to me more than once that that isn't the case.

My heart goes crazy the moment Aston sits up and kisses my forehead, before he stands to his feet.

"How about we get some fresh air, talk out on the porch?"

I sit up and smile. "Yeah, okay." I want to talk to Aston, want to get to know him more, to have him know more about me.

I get off the couch, and we head toward the back of the house. I notice he grabs his guitar one the way out.

Once we're sitting down, he looks over at me, this intensity on his face, but this softness comes through when our eyes meet.

"Tell me what makes you happy," he says the sincerity in his voice not masked by the harshness that is all Aston.

I glance up at the sky, the stars so bright among the darkness.

"I've never really thought about it," I answer honestly. I think about his question, about when I was truly, really happy. "Melissa has always made me happy. She's my best friend, but you know who really makes me happy?" I glance at him.

He's picking at his guitar, but I can tell he's listening to me.

"You make me happy. So happy, Aston, and that kind of scares me."

He sets his guitar down, and before I know what he's doing, he's pulling me onto his lap.

I rest against his chest, his body big and warm, hard and masculine.

"You make me fucking happy too, more than I ever thought possible in my life."

I smile at that, knowing how he feels. It's how I feel, too.

"Tell me about your mom? Tell me what happened to her."

He squeezes me tighter to him, his warm lips brushing against my neck as he speaks again. "Tell me everything I should know about you. I want to learn every fucking thing."

Closing my eyes, I lean my head back and rest it against his shoulder. "My mother was mentally ill. Severe depression and anxiety that no pills seemed to fully control. She'd been through a lot in her life that no one understood, and when you live in a small town . . . people talk." I stop to release a small breath, thinking about how damn much I miss her. "It got so bad that my father up and left her with barely even a good-bye. Left us both as if we were nothing, and eventually she realized she couldn't handle being here any longer. She couldn't handle being in her own head, and she took her own life."

A tear slides down my cheek the moment Aston's lips gently press against my neck to comfort me. "I'm sorry, baby. Sometimes a person's own mind is their worst enemy. I know that feeling all too well, and it can consume you, making it so damn hard to breathe."

"It's been over a year now," I continue. "I stayed in town at first, trying my best to move on with everyday activities, but it became overwhelming with everyone around me always bringing her up and making snide remarks about her death." A small breath escapes me when I feel Aston's thumb run across my cheek, swiping the tear away.

I take a few seconds to regain my composure before I attempt to go on. "Melissa kept telling me to move in with her and forget about our hometown. Finally, I found my way here. So here I am. Here with you under the stars."

"I'm so fucking happy you listened to Melissa." He kisses my neck again and buries his face in it, his arms holding me protectively. "Remind me to thank that roommate of yours one day. Fuck, I owe her for bringing you here."

For long moments we stay this way, the remembrance of the soft tune he'd been strumming filling my head and the stillness of the night surrounding me as he holds me.

But as I feel myself drifting off, feeling so comfortable in his arms, the sound of tires crunching on the gravel driveway rouses me.

"What the fuck?" Aston says, his voice harsh, dangerous.

We rise and walk around the house when we hear what sounds like a truck approaching. By the way Aston pushes me behind his back and how tense he's become, I'm going to assume this is some bad shit.

Aston

THE TRUCK COMES TO A stop in front of the house, and I know that this isn't going to be a good fucking night.

I recognize the truck from the house across from where Melissa lives, and know the fuckers we offered a beat down to have decided to come back for a little vengeance.

I had a feeling they'd want to retaliate, especially when I noticed that fucker watching Kadence's house. I just had no idea they'd actually have the balls to do it.

But only one guy gets out of the car—at first, anyway. The tinted windows make it hard to see if there's more inside, but this fucker would have to have a death wish to come alone.

It's the same prick who'd been mean-mugging me the whole time I fucking watched his ass at Kadence's house.

It's the same fucker who I beat the shit out of and smashed his face into the arm of the couch.

I might need to call my brothers. I can handle this prick, even his asshole friends if one chooses to join him. But any more and there will be trouble, a lot of fucking trouble.

That's when I'll need my sadistic brothers.

"Hey, remember me, you fucking asshole?"

"Go inside, Kadence." I hope she actually fucking listens to me. I'm thankful as hell when I hear her close the door behind her.

I stare at the asshole in front of me and notice the gun he's got in his hand. It's close to his body, and from the way he's tense, his finger twitching on the side of the gun, I'm almost positive he's never actually fired the thing in his life.

That makes for a pretty dangerous situation. He's working on emotion, and although that might make him sloppy, it might also make him unstable . . . even more so than he was.

"You made a huge fucking mistake by coming here. You know that, right, motherfucker?"

He grins, trying to keep his grip on the pistol firm, but I can see his hand shaking. This kid doesn't want to use that thing.

Hell, maybe he doesn't have to.

Reaching for my guitar, I grin and walk down the steps, keeping my eyes steady on his, knowing that I'm intimidating him.

It's then that I hear one of his asshole friends coming at me from the side. The prick tried to be slick by walking the property instead of arriving in the truck.

Too bad for them King is out walking the property and will hunt them down real fucking soon. This one got lucky to get past him unnoticed.

Knowing this could possibly be a huge fucking mistake, I take my eyes off the kid with the gun and slam my guitar into the other guy's face, knocking him down into the dirt.

I take my anger out on his face, slamming my broken guitar into him repeatedly until his face is covered in blood and the knife he was holding slips out of his hand, allowing me to kick it away.

Turning back around, I toss the guitar down and come at pistol kid before he can get brave enough to use that thing.

I hear the sound go off right before I feel the bullet slam into my shoulder, pain spreading throughout my arm, stunning me for a short moment.

This has Kadence rushing out of the house to make sure I'm not dead. I immediately push her behind me to keep her out of his shooting range, but before I can react, she's holding out the pistol I had sitting downstairs on my bed, and aiming it at the guy.

I don't know what in the fuck is going on, but my girl is fierce as fuck. Maybe a little too fierce.

"Put the gun down, or I won't hesitate to use this thing." She takes a step closer to him, but I quickly throw my uninjured arm out, keeping her back. I can feel her body shaking, but I can tell by the tone of her voice that she means business. "I mean it. Do it! Don't even think for one second that I would hesitate to put a bullet in your chest."

As much as I love the fact that she's just as willing to protect me as I am her, I couldn't let her pull that trigger even if she wanted to.

This is my life. It's the life me and my brothers chose. There's no way in hell I'm letting her get her hands dirty to save my ass.

Holding my shoulder, I keep my eye on the fucker, taking in every movement he makes, waiting for just the right time to make my move.

"Nah-ah. Nope." He waves the gun at us while talking. "This

motherfucker and his brothers came into *my* house, roughed us up, took our money, and broke fucking bones. No one does that shit and gets away with it. Locke brothers or not. Well tell me, motherfucker . . ." He cocks back the hammer and begins walking toward us. "Where are your brothers to fight now?"

The closer he gets, I can see the sweat trickling down his forehead, this asshole clearly not confident with that pistol he's aiming at me. Maybe worried that even that won't be enough to save him.

And if his friends don't come out to help him soon, worrying is what he *should* be doing.

"Stop walking!" Kadence shouts. "Right now, damn it!"

This has the asshole laughing, throwing him off his game. If you're going to use a gun, you should know to never take your eye off the enemy, not even for a split fucking second.

He made a mistake with that, giving me just the time I need to take charge of this situation before he can put another bullet in me or, hell, Kadence.

Quickly, I snatch the pistol from Kadence's hand and stalk toward him, pressing the barrel right between his eyes.

I push past the pain, ignore it as I focus on this bastard.

"Who said I need my brothers?"

Truth is I wish I had my brothers here, but if this fucker thinks I can't handle him on my own, I'm about to show him exactly how fucking crazy I am.

"Kadence," I growl. "Get back inside and lock the fucking doors. Now."

She says no at first, but finally takes a few steps back toward the house once she hears King's bark coming from somewhere down by the river.

Ace comes from out of nowhere, dragging another one of the assholes by his neck as if he's a rag doll.

Once she sees that one of my brothers have now joined me, she rushes into the house and locks the door as told.

I warned this motherfucker that coming here was a huge mistake.

He's about to see just how fucking huge.

Now it's time to push that point home.

Kadence

I DON'T KNOW WHAT THE hell came over me, but when I heard that gunshot, fear of losing Aston took over and before I knew it, I was rushing outside with Aston's pistol in my hand.

As soon as he sent me inside the first time, I ran down to his room, knowing there'd be a gun on his bed. I remembered seeing it before we got comfortable on the couch earlier.

Melissa would kill me if she knew I'd risked my life for Aston tonight—risked my life in general—and that I'm hiding out in the Locke house while there's a possible war breaking loose just outside.

I'm not going to lie; I'm terrified. Terrified for Aston and his brothers, although I have a feeling I shouldn't be.

The whole town knows how dangerous the Locke brothers are. They can handle themselves, and I'm pretty sure this can't be the worst situation they've been in.

Still, I can't stop my body from shaking as I think of the worst possible scenario. The thought of losing Aston has my stomach rolling, feeling as if I'm about to lose my dinner.

It's quiet outside. Too quiet, as if they've somehow managed to take this situation away from the house. Possibly into the woods, where I know their pit bull got ahold of one of those assholes attempting to sneak around the property.

Who knows how many more are out there. They're most likely outnumbered.

Twenty minutes go by. Then forty, before I finally hear someone yanking on the door handle, trying to pry it open.

My heart sinks, my stomach twisting into nervous knots until I hear Sterling's voice, telling me to unlock the door.

Before I know it, I'm standing in front of the door, pulling it open to see Sterling and Ace looking back at me, both of them splattered with blood and looking a bit roughed up.

Panic immediately starts to kick in, my worry for Aston taking over until he rounds the corner, smiling up at me as if to tell me not to worry.

On instinct I rush over to him and throw my arms around his neck, crushing my lips to his.

He kisses me back hard, so fucking hard that I somehow end up biting my bottom lip.

Once we pull away from the kiss, he cups my face, his gaze meeting mine. "Don't ever risk your life for me again, Kadence. Yours is worth so much more than mine ever could be. Got it?"

"You might have the whole world fooled," I say while keeping my eyes locked with his beautiful blue ones, "but not me. I see the real you. I *feel* the real you, and it's so much better than you think. Don't ever tell me you're not worth it."

"All right, time to break this mushy shit up and get this damn bullet out of your arm, little brother." Sterling slaps him on the back and flashes me a smile. "You're one badass chick. Looks like you're more than capable of handling a Locke. Just do us all a favor and don't get yourself killed." He winks and calls for Ace to join him in a different room, where I'm guessing they plan to take care of Aston's shoulder.

What in the hell have I gotten myself into?

But even thinking that, I can't help but smile.

Aston

I HEAR THE SOUND OF the bullet hitting the sink, smell the blood filling the air, and feel the tugging as Ace bandages the wound up.

"All right, you're good, little brother." Ace secures the bandage and steps back with a smirk, proud of his handiwork.

"You're not going to the hospital?" Kadence says with shock in her voice, looking between the three of us.

Sterling is the one to speak. "It's a gunshot wound. That would draw too much attention. It went in clean, and we'll watch it. He'll be fine. You're both lucky as fuck we pulled up when we did, but just remember our job is to protect *you*. You're one of us now, Kadence, but that doesn't mean you fight for us. When things get dirty, you run, got it? Plain and simple."

Kadence nods her head, offering a small smile, seeming pleased to be called one of us.

"Good. We'll leave you."

Ace and Sterling leave, and I stare at Kadence, taking in her expression.

"I'm fine, baby." I can see she's worried, so I pull her in and hold her, wanting nothing more than to comfort her. This woman that was willing to risk her fucking life for me.

"That was insane," she whispers.

"Yeah, it was. I wish you hadn't been involved." I pull her back and look into her eyes. "Sterling was right. You may be one of us, but I never want to see you out there on the battlefield again. Let *us* protect you and never the other way around. Promise me." My voice is hard, wanting her to know how damn serious I am. "Fucking promise me now."

"I promise," she says, a little breathless as her eyes search mine.

I might be wounded, but I need her right now, need to touch her, hold her, feel her. I need to know this is real, that she's not going anywhere.

Maybe she needs this moment as much as I do. It sure as hell feels like it, and when it comes to Kadence, I haven't been wrong yet.

A second later we're kissing, my tongue between her lips, my body pressed to hers.

A small noise leaves her, this one of want, of need . . . of being here with me.

Has me so fucking hard.

I can't help the small noise that leaves me. She just feels too fucking good.

She breaks the kiss, panting.

"No, you're injured. Let's just rest, talk."

But the way she looks at me after I grin tells me she knows I'm not about to let this end.

Kadence

WE NEED TO STOP THIS because Aston needs to rest. But he's alive and I want him. I want to feel him, to know he's here with me.

He's on me, pulling me closer, kissing me again until we're somehow making our way downstairs, our mouths barely leaving each other's.

I'm lost in the sensations, making it impossible for me to resist him, wounded or not. Doesn't matter; I will *always* want this man.

We go to the bed, he lays me on it, his big body over mine, and I just absorb the feelings.

He starts to kiss and suck the side of my neck, completely ignoring the pain in his shoulder as if I'm all he cares about. Aston is thorough with his tongue and lips, making me squirm beneath him, ready to beg for his cock in me.

I try not to touch his shoulder, but I want to feel his heat, his strength. I want to know that this moment is happening.

The hot, hard length of him is between my thighs. He starts moving his hips back and forth, rubbing himself against me.

"I need you out of these fucking clothes," he growls next to my ear. "Get them off."

I don't wait for him to ask twice.

Sitting up, I strip myself of my shirt and pants before reaching over and gently pulling Aston's shirt up his body, until I'm tossing it on the floor next to mine.

I reach for his pants, to undo them, but Aston makes it hard, his mouth capturing mine and biting as I struggle to undress us both, until we're both finally free of our clothing and panting into each other's mouths.

I look down as much as I can, and with the way Aston hovers over me, I can see his cock sliding through my cleft. It's so damn arousing, and I know I can get off from this alone.

His cockhead moves against my clit every time he presses his dick upward. I groan at how good it feels, wanting and needing it inside of me before I go crazy with this need.

"How much do you want me?" he whispers against my lips while wrapping his hand around my throat. He gives it a gentle squeeze and moves his cock against me again. "How fucking much?"

I want to feel him stretching me, pushing into me hard. I want to feel like what happened, him getting hurt, nearly dying, was a dream.

A nightmare.

He starts to swirl his tongue around the shell of my ear, causing my lips to part and my eyes to close.

"I need you in me, now."

Without breaking away, Aston releases my throat and reaches between our bodies, grabs his cock, and places the tip at the entrance of my pussy.

Everything inside of me stills, my hands gripping his back, preparing for his intrusion. For his thickness to fill me, to consume me.

"I can't go slow. The thought of you getting hurt or killed because of me makes me fucking insane. I'm about to show you just how much I need you."

All I can do is nod and hold on tight, more than ready to take him, to feel him. Everything he has to give me.

In one deep, hard thrust he shoves his thickness into me, causing me to scream and dig my nails into his muscular back. His balls are pressed right up against my body once he buries himself all the way inside me. I am stretched to the max, the pain mixing with the pleasure, making me hungry for more.

"Fuck," he says harshly. He pushes in and out, over and over, groaning with every thrust and retreat.

I scream against his sweaty neck, holding on for dear life as he takes me hard. Fast and hard, as if he needs to be inside me to survive. As if we need each other to breathe. And in this moment, I do.

I lift my gaze to his abdomen, seeing his six-pack clench and relax with every thrust. He slams his pelvis against mine, the sound of sloppy sex so arousing.

With just a few more hard thrusts from Aston, I'm coming around his cock, scraping my nails down his back, most likely drawing blood.

This has Aston growling into my neck, his hands gripping me anywhere he can as he continues to pound into me until I feel his cum filling me once again.

"You're so fucking perfect, Kadence." He slams into me and stops. "And you're mine."

Kadence

WE SPEND THE NEXT COUPLE of hours alternating between fucking and catching our breath, until we finally find ourselves lying in his bed, him holding me as he talks about his old life.

The one he had before his parents got murdered.

Hearing all the stories of how his parents hurt their children rips my heart out, only giving me more of an understanding of the lives of the Locke boys.

I can't even imagine going my whole childhood afraid of what my parents might do next. Afraid of what new way they might find to physically hurt or torture me.

It wasn't until their uncle Killian, found out and stepped in that the boys moved into the safety of his home.

The boys should've been safe then, but their parents always found some way to manipulate the boys out of their uncle's house and back with them, until the process started all over again.

Aston was just moving of his parents' house for the fourth and final time when he stopped at home late at night to pack his belongings. He found his parents murdered and two dealers robbing them of anything of worth.

The dealers assumed he was alone and stabbed him three times, leaving him for dead, but Sterling and Ace were just outside, smoking a joint and waiting for him.

As soon as they saw the dealers running from the front door, they rushed into the house to find Aston on the floor, bleeding to death.

Sterling took care of Aston until the ambulance arrived, while Ace tracked down the dealers and made them pay.

He killed them both without question, and I have a feeling that when it comes to protecting each other, that they'd kill every single time.

The Locke brothers have been hard and cold ever since, not letting fear cripple them anymore.

"I don't know what to say," I whisper into Aston's neck. "I hate that you almost died. That you could've died tonight too. The thought kills me, Aston. I can't lose you. I won't."

He pulls me onto his hard chest and kisses my forehead, giving me the reassurance I need right now. "That shit ain't going to happen. Nothing is going to fucking keep me from you. Ever. Never forget that. I don't give a shit what it takes. I'll never stop fighting when it comes to being with you."

His words relax me, causing me to fall further into him, allowing his embrace to comfort me. "I hope so," I say gently. "I'm in too deep with you now."

"Me too, baby. Me too."

I practically jump out of Aston's arms when there's a loud bang on his bedroom door.

"Holy shit!" I grab my chest and bury myself under the sheet.

I feel Aston laugh against my arm before he pulls me back to him and yells to whoever's knocking on the door. "What do you want, asshole?"

"We need to discuss some shit," Sterling yells back. "Get dressed and come upstairs. You've got five minutes or we're coming to you."

"Fuck." Aston sits up and runs his hands through his slick hair. "He's right. Even though we roughed these motherfuckers up and showed them we're not to be messed with, we need to come up with a solution for you and your roommate. These guys weren't playing. They came here ready to take us out and hurt us in any way possible. It nearly took Ace drowning a motherfucker to get them to finally back off and leave, agreeing to our terms if we took it easy on them. Still, I don't trust them."

We both crawl out of bed and begin getting dressed. I can see how tense Aston is, as if he's busy thinking about me getting hurt.

"We're gonna need to find you guys somewhere else to live. It needs to be somewhere safe and closer to us so we can keep an eye out on you two better. Even though we made it clear we wanted those fuckers out of town by tonight, you can never be too safe."

Aston grabs my hand, keeping me close. I follow him upstairs to where his brothers are eating a pizza and chilling on the couch as if they hadn't just almost killed or gotten killed.

Aston didn't go into detail about what happened out there, besides Ace almost drowning someone, and honestly I don't want to know. Their enemies were out for blood when they arrived, but the three Locke brothers are still breathing. All I care about is that the boys took care of them before they were able to take care of the Locke brothers.

Ace pats the seat next to him and gives me a sexy little wink. "Sit. Have some pizza."

I get ready to sit down, but Aston sits first, pulling me into his lap and wrapping his strong arms around me. "All right. Let's discuss this shit so I can get my girl back to bed. It's late."

Sterling shakes his head and hands me a slice of pizza, which I take and begin eating. It's well past two now, and suddenly my stomach is growling.

"I called Uncle Killian, and he's looking into a few properties nearby that we can get our hands on. Said he might have some connections. We should have word within a few days." Sterling tosses his pizza down and gives me a stern look. "I'm sure Aston already told you the plan. It's better to be safe than sorry. Being sorry isn't something us Lockes do very well. We need you to do this for us. Got it?"

I nod my head and lean into Aston as he holds me tighter to him to comfort me and let me know that I'm safe in the hands of him and his brothers.

My safety isn't something I'm concerned about when it comes to the Lockes. It's getting Melissa to agree that worries me.

She already hates the idea of the Lockes even coming close to our house. I can't imagine how she's going to take us needing to move next to them and into their safety.

"I'll talk to my roommate tomorrow and let her know what the plan is. It's going to take some convincing to get her to agree, but I'm down for anything that you guys feel is safe for us. I trust you guys, and I'm going to do my best to get her to as well."

"Good." Sterling stands up and hands me a beer. "Welcome

to the circle."

I feel Aston smile against my neck before he kisses his way up it. A small moan escapes me, causing him to growl into my ear.

"Finish that beer so I can take you back to my bed. I'm not done with you yet. I won't be for a long fucking time."

Holy fuck . . . I don't want him to be. Ever.

One week later . . .

I STARE AT MELISSA AND Kadence as they argue over what they need to keep and what needs to get trashed.

They've been doing this for the last three hours, and I have to admit that it's been quite amusing.

Her roommate wasn't comfortable with us helping them move at first, but after I made it clear that there was no way in hell we weren't helping, she calmed down a bit, allowing us to touch her things.

Doesn't mean she hasn't been watching our every move from the corner of her eye as if she expects us to bite her or some shit.

I am a possessive bastard when it comes to Kadence.

I don't fucking deny that.

Her friend Melissa is important in her life, and although I don't want Kadence staying right across the street from the assholes we sent away, I'm not going to leave her friend high and dry and put her in potential danger.

So we helped them find a place closer to us with the assistance of Killian. It's nicer, not near where those fuckers lived, and I'm five damn minutes from Kadence.

Sterling and I are helping them move, and Ace is setting up some security shit at their new place. Can never be too cautious when it comes to the safety of my girl. Even with having her close, you never know what the fuck could happen.

There's some pretty fucked-up people in this town.

I assumed Melissa would have been totally against this whole idea, but once we told her what had gone down with those fuckers, me getting shot, and Kadence in danger, she was more than willing to pack up and move where it was safe. Apparently she just wasn't expecting us to physically be here helping.

"One last time, ladies." Sterling holds up an ugly old lamp that looks like it was salvaged from the dumpster. "Is this shit coming with or staying? Please tell me this ugly fucker is going in the trash."

"Staying," Kadence says quickly before Melissa can respond. "Staying."

"I like it, but fine." Melissa rolls her eyes at Kadence. "Toss the damn thing. Less junk to unpack."

Sterling grins and throws his cigarette down. "Good fucking choice. This is the most hideous thing I've ever seen." He kicks the lamp across the yard and jumps up to close the back of the truck. "I'm gonna do one more sweep to make sure those assholes are really gone and not just hiding out. I'll meet you at the girls'."

I nod my head and turn to the girls. "You two ready to roll?"

Kadence and Melissa stop by the moving truck, look back at the house, and then glance at me.

"As ready as we will be," Kadence says, and I pull her into the hardness of my body, reminding her that I'll do anything to protect her.

She's one of us now. She's mine and I protect what is mine, no matter the consequences.

"Then let's roll."

EPILOGUE

Kadence

Six months later

I STARE AT THE BONFIRE in the center of the Locke brothers' property and smile. Aston is beside me, his new guitar in hand as he strums on it.

The sound is peaceful, lulling almost.

I've gotten so used to this that I'm not sure what it would feel like not to be here right now, under the stars with the Locke brothers.

It's something we've been doing every Saturday for the last six months. Even on the colder nights, we still find our way out here in the stillness of the night sitting around a fire having drinks and just giving each other hell.

The boys have been doing this for years now. It's their way of letting each other know that they're a family and nothing will ever break them apart.

It's their short moment of peace in the chaos of their lives. If it weren't for these moments, then I'm more than positive they'd lose their shit.

"You fucker," Ace says to Sterling while elbowing him hard in the chest. "Get your own beer. You saw my ass just grab that one and set it down."

Sterling holds up the bottle with a cocky grin. "You know what happens when you leave shit sitting around. Becomes available to the first motherfucker to grab it."

Ace reaches under his chair for another beer. "It's cool." He pops the top and sits back. "Good thing I'm always prepared."

I start to laugh because this is pretty typical of these guys. And to be honest I'm loving it. I feel like I'm at home, like they are my family.

It's a damn good feeling.

I glance at Melissa, who over the last few months has actually warmed up to the idea of hanging out with them. This is the eighth bonfire she's joined us for, and she seems to fight less and less with each time I ask her to come.

She was still hesitant at first. But she saw how much Aston cared about me, and how much I do for him. She realized this is my life now.

Aston is the man I love. He's where I feel the safest.

"Beer?" Aston hands me one, and I smile and grab it. Before I can take a drink, he grabs my face and kisses me hard, reminding me, just like every day, that I'm his.

I love that about Aston. He's not afraid to show me every single day that I'm his and he'll do anything for me. It doesn't matter what it is, anything I ever fucking ask—although I try not to ask for much.

Truthfully all I want is for him to be there for me, and that's something I know he'll always be. He's proved that every day for over six months, and I've done everything I can to do the same for him.

Leaning against him, I tilt my beer back, taking a small sip. It's cold and runs down my throat, this hoppy, bitter taste that covers my tongue.

I watch the flames again, wondering how my life ended up here. I love it, I really do. I feel like I've finally found my family, like what I was given in life led up to this moment.

"Chug, little sister," Sterling says with a grin.

I smile, the endearment hitting my heart. They welcome me, see me as their family, too.

I glance at Melissa, and see she's grinning. I'm glad she came around and is happy hanging with us, being around them.

She's my family too, my sister, and without her in my life I would be lost.

"Come here, baby," Aston says and pulls me into his lap, his strong arms holding me protectively.

"Come on, chug, Kadence. There are a lot more beers to go around, and this night isn't over until they're all fucking gone." Ace tilts back his beer right before he falls to the ground from Sterling kicking his chair over. "Fucker," he growls before placing the beer back to his lips and taking a drink anyways. "I can drink from here just fine."

"Ignore them and kiss me," Aston says, and before I can do or say anything, he's kissing me, making everything else around us disappear. His mouth on mine always seems to do that. Makes me feel as if it's just the two of us. No one has ever been able to make me feel this happy, and I know from the way he treats me, like I'm his fucking everything, that no one has ever made him feel this happy either.

"I love you," he whispers against my lips. "Do you fucking know that?"

My breath hitches in my throat from his confession, and heat swarms throughout my whole body, making me feel as if I've just burst into flames.

I can hardly breathe, to be honest.

Aston Locke loves me, and I have a feeling that's something he doesn't feel for many people other than his brothers and uncle.

I've known I loved him for a while, but hearing him say it first has my heart beating straight out of my chest.

I love this man so fucking much that it hurts. Belonging to Aston is everything I could've ever asked for.

Aston

KADENCE'S BREATHING PICKS UP AGAINST my lips, letting me know that my confession has her heart and body reacting.

Good. That's real fucking good.

It lets me know that she loves me too. Even if she doesn't say it back. She doesn't need to.

I feel it with every moment we spend together.

Every touch.

Every kiss.

Every time I'm inside her.

Kadence is mine, and I've known it from the moment our eyes first locked that night across from her house.

Smiling, she leans into me, gently brushing her lips over mine. "Guess what?"

"What?" I whisper while running my thumb over her cheekbone. "Tell me."

"I love you too, Aston."

Feeling overwhelmed with emotions, I grip the back of her head and kiss her so fucking hard that it hurts.

I kiss her until we're both fighting for air and one of my brothers is throwing something at us to break it up.

Doesn't matter.

They can throw shit at me all night, and I'd kiss this woman until I can't breathe. I wouldn't stop until I knew she needed to come up for air.

"Holy shit, little brother."

I glance at Ace.

He jumps up from his spot on the ground. "Did I just hear you say love?"

"Hell yeah, you did," Sterling says with a smile. "Our littlest Locke has found his woman."

"Well, I know that shit. But that dipshit has barely even said he loves us. This calls for a cele-fucking-bration."

Ace disappears into the house and comes out a few seconds later with some guns and moonshine.

This motherfucker . . .

"You don't have to drink that shit." I laugh against Kadence's lips. "Even I think that crap taste like shit."

She leans in and bites my lip. I love it when she does that.

It reminds me that she doesn't give a shit who's around us. She wants me and she's not afraid to show it.

Standing up, I grab Kadence and throw her over my shoulder, giving her ass a hard smack.

"Oh come on!" Melissa laughs while holding up a beer. "You're going to leave me out here with the two craziest Lockes?"

I smirk. "She'll be back . . . in a few hours."

I'm just about to escape inside with Kadence so we can get a little time alone when a set of headlights has us all looking down the driveway.

I instantly set Kadence down and stand in front of her, while Ace pushes Melissa behind him. None of us know what to expect.

But from his expression, Sterling recognizes the little white car the second it pulls up and the engine cuts off.

We all watch as a petite brunette steps out and closes the door behind her. It's not until she walks closer to the fire that I realize it's Sterling's old crush from high school . . . a girl I know Sterling has still kept in contact with. A girl Sterling still cares about.

Wynter's face is busted up, causing Sterling to immediately throw his bottle of beer at the house and walk over to her, pulling her into his chest as she cries into him.

Looks like some whole new shit is about to happen.

There's no way my brother will allow the asshole that hurt her to get away with it.

I love Kadence, and I'd do anything for my girl. Same goes for my brothers, and I know Wynter is the one that got away for Sterling.

The one girl he always wanted but never quite got.

And so it continues.

The dark, twisted ways of the fucking Locke brothers.

THE END

Coming soon

SAVAGE LOCKE

(LOCKE BROTHERS, 2)

Turn the page to read the first two chapters of HARD AND RECKLESS by Victoria Ashley.

HARD AND RECKLESS
CHAPTER ONE

Jameson Daniels

WRAPPING AN ARM AROUND MY neck, Katie stands to her tiptoes and presses her lips against mine, before pulling away with a sexy little laugh. "Here you are. Thought you got lost. It's been close to an hour since I've seen you."

Growling, I lift her off her feet, and roughly bite her bottom lip, before moving around to speak against her ear. "I'm always around, baby. Just got a little busy talking about club security. I'll meet you downstairs in a minute. Just need to change first."

With a small moan, Katie releases my neck and slowly runs her hands down my chest and abs, stopping at my belt and tugging on it. "Alright, but hurry. I've been waiting all night to get my greedy little hands on you and have you to myself."

I roughly cup the back of her head, placing my forehead to hers. "Keep talking like that and I'll bend you over the railing right now and fuck you. I don't care that my house is full of people. You know me."

"Mmm . . ." she moans. "Sounds tempting."

"Hey, man. I need you for a minute."

Pulling my forehead away from Katie's, I look over to see Rowdy standing in the hallway with a drink in hand. He's a good friend of mine and another security guard at the nightclub I work at. That's exactly why I like having him around when I decide to throw a party here. More help keeping the people under control when needed. "What's up, Rowdy? Everything okay downstairs?"

He shakes his head. "Nah, I need to talk to you in private. Now."

Katie groans and kisses my cheek. "This is going to be a looong night." Smiling, she gently slaps Rowdy's cheek. "Don't keep my man busy for too long, handsome. I need him if you know what I mean."

Rowdy looks tense, but doesn't say a word as he watches Katie walk away. "Let's go back to the game room," he says stiffly.

He doesn't even wait for me to respond, before he walks away with purpose. Has me thinking that something major is happening.

I don't like that feeling one bit. Has me on edge, ready for something to go down.

Once we get inside the room, I shut the door behind me and walk over to lean against the table. "Alright, well what the hell is going on?"

He runs his ink covered hands down his face and mumbles, making it hard for me to understand what he's saying. "Cole is fucking Katie."

Rage courses through me, causing my blood to boil, as I demand Rowdy to repeat the words that just left his mouth.

I'm hoping like hell that I heard wrong, because I'd hate to have to kill my best friend tonight.

"What the fuck did you just say?"

I grip the table behind me, feeling the veins in my neck begin to throb as I wait for him to speak again. Feels like the longest ten seconds of my life.

"Wait. Shit, I need this first." Holding up his finger, he takes a long swig of his vodka and leans against the wall, before pulling out a joint and lighting it. He takes two quick hits, before blowing out a cloud of smoke. "Cole is *fucking* your girl. They're sneaking around behind your damn back, man." His eyes meet mine, showing me just how gone he is right now. Even high and completely wasted though, he knows that's something you don't fuck around with me about.

"How sure are you?" I growl out, squeezing the table tighter. Something's about to break soon. Probably my damn hand at this rate. "You better be damn fucking sure, Rowdy and not just assuming."

Flexing his jaw, he downs the rest of his drink and then slams the empty glass down next to him, looking pissed that I would even question him. "I wouldn't come to you out of a damn assumption, asshole. I saw the two of them sneak out of the guest room together, looking thoroughly fucked. I wasn't quite as drunk ten minutes ago, but seeing one of my best fucking friends sneak around with my other best friend's girl, had me downing a few shots on the way to find your ass."

Pushing away from the table, I turn around and flip it over, before running my hands over my face and yelling, "Fuuuuck!"

I've never felt so betrayed in my life and there's not a damn word that can explain how I truly feel right now. Over twenty years of friendship with Cole and this is the shit I get. He sleeps with my girlfriend of four fucking years.

"I'd be pissed too, man," Rowdy says from across the room as I pace, trying to gather my thoughts and piece this shit together. "Cole just broke the bro code and in your house to top that shit off. That's messed up. I'd kill him."

My heart is racing so fast that I need to get out of here, before I explode and take it out on the wrong person. My chest is tight and I can't think straight. None of his words seem to make sense right now. All I feel in this moment is pure hatred.

"Where is he?" I stop pacing to look at him. "Is that piece of shit still downstairs?"

"Nah, man. I saw him walk out the door right when I got up here to find you. He left about five minutes ago."

Cracking my neck, I reach for my jacket and slip it on, before reaching for my helmet. "Watch my house and keep everyone in check until I get back. Don't let anyone upstairs."

"You're gonna chase him down and beat–"

"Damn straight, I am," I say, cutting him off as I rush out the door, headed on a mission. Cole might've left five minutes ago, but I'm faster and more reckless.

"Jameson!" Katie rushes out of the kitchen, grabbing my arm, once I make it downstairs. "Where are you going? Everything okay?"

I yank my arm away, clenching my jaw, as I stop to look at her. She's beautiful as hell, but it's not worth trying to fix this shit. Fuck me over once and you're done. "To find Cole." Feeling my chest ache, I lean in close to speak against her ear. It's the closest I'll ever get to her again. "Get the fuck out of my house. We're done."

The color drains from her face, realization finally kicking in, that I know about her and Cole.

"Jameson, wait!" She attempts to grab my arm again, but I shake it off and push my way through the crowd, needing to get to Cole.

I can hear Katie following behind me, yelling for me to let her explain, but all I see is red as I straddle my Hayabusa and start the engine.

Cole lives less than fifteen minutes from me, so I have about seven minutes to catch him, before he makes it home for the night.

Shoving my helmet on, I rev the engine and speed off, leaving Katie to scream and cry after me, asking for something that I'll never give her: a second chance.

Leaning forward, I weave my way through traffic, speeding pass vehicles, while on the lookout for Cole's car.

After a while, I spot him two stoplights ahead of me, so I turn off at an alley that I know leads to where Cole is headed.

Speeding up, I fight to control my breathing, but all I can think about is my best friend between my girl's legs, fucking her and making her scream. It only makes it harder to breathe.

Reaching the end of the alley, I turn left, heading toward the side street that I know Cole will be approaching from any second now.

As expected, Cole's black Dodge Challenger, comes into view, making me speed up along the side to pass him.

Pulling out in front of him, once I give myself enough room, my bike skids to a stop, causing Cole to honk the horn and slam on his brakes, almost hitting me.

I don't even care at this point. Him hitting me would only give me more reason to kill his *Don Juan* ass.

After a few seconds, he pushes his door open and steps out of the car, looking me over as if I'm crazy. "What the fuck, Jameson!" He closes the driver door behind him, before throwing his arms up and walking closer to me. "What the hell is your problem? I could've killed your ass. Or shit. Even my damn self. I'm too fucking sexy to die, man," he shouts. "The female population would be left devastated and it would be your fault."

Kicking my stand down, I jump off my bike and pull my helmet off, tossing it at the road.

That's when I see it register on his face that he knows *exactly* what my problem is.

"Good thing you didn't." Clenching my jaw, I step up in his face and crack my neck, locking my eyes with his dark ones. "Then I wouldn't get to do this to you for *fucking* my girl."

Swinging out, I punch him in the mouth, causing him to stumble back, before I quickly swing my elbow out, connecting it with his jaw.

This causes him to fall back, but he quickly recovers, jumping back up to his feet and looking me over, with heavy breaths.

His jaw flexes as if he wants to swing back, but he doesn't. Maybe it's because he knows he deserves that and much more.

"Fuck!" Wiping his thumb over his bloody mouth, he cusses to himself, while cracking his neck. "That's some fucked up shit! All over a girl, too? Katie isn't right for you. Never has been. I did you a favor. Open your fucking eyes."

"Fuuck! Always over a girl, Cole." I step up until we're nose to nose, so he can feel my anger with each breath. "Especially when that girl is *mine*. No one fucking touches what is mine."

With that, I grab his throat and squeeze, causing him to growl out as if he wants to rip my throat out just as badly as I want to his. "We've been friends for over twenty years, but fuck me over again and I *will* kill your ass." I slam him down onto the hood of his car and squeeze his neck tighter. "I'll never forget this shit, asshole. This is the worst way to break my fucking trust."

Releasing his neck, I step away from him and bend down to pick up my helmet, before walking back over to hop on my bike. If I have to look at him for another second, I have no idea what I'll end up doing to him.

I hear him coming up behind me as I slip the helmet on and breathe heavily into it. "That's it?" he questions, throwing his arms out and circling around my bike. "We're not going to talk about this shit so I can explain? I wouldn't just fuck your girl without good reason. You know me better than that. You're like a brother to me. Hell . . . you are my brother."

I rev the engine and look him up and down, standing there with his tattooed fists clenched at his sides. "No, I *thought* I knew you better than that. Your words don't mean shit, so don't bother coming around for a while. This was *nothing* compared to what I really want to do to you. Consider yourself lucky, motherfucker."

Gripping the handle bars, tightly, I take off, finding open road for me to cut loose on, so I can calm down enough, before returning to my party.

I'm usually good at being in control. But not tonight . . . Cole has me all worked up.

This is beyond fucked up on so many levels. Cole's always been the playboy type when it comes to women, but I never in a million years thought he'd pull that shit with my girl.

I thought he knew better than to fuck me over.

I was wrong.

After driving around for thirty minutes, I call Rowdy and tell him I'm on my way and I'll deal with Katie when I get there.

Apparently, after I left, Rowdy tried making her leave, and she got mad, swinging at him.

So, he threw his hands up and backed away, letting her get a few hits to his chest to calm her down.

I'm gonna owe him later for taking a few hits for me.

When I pull up outside my house, Katie is sitting on the porch, but she stands up immediately, when she hears me coming.

The sight of her walking toward me has me tightening my jaw as I take my helmet off, and get off my bike.

"It was just this once, I swear. It'll never happen again. All the other rumors about me aren't true though. You've got to believe me. I'd never hurt you on purpose. I'm just . . . I've been drinking. I wasn't thinking clearly." She grabs my arm and pulls on it, when I just keep on walking. "Will you stop for two fucking seconds and talk to me!"

"Stop with the fucking excuses." Taking a deep breath, I stop walking and look down at her, as she stands in front of me, pushing on my chest to keep me from moving. "Your words mean nothing," I bark. "It's your actions that speak, but you just showed me that trusting you was a mistake."

Her face is red from crying, so I turn away, not letting her tears sway me to change my mind. I know she's not drunk. She might forget how well I fucking know her. She knew perfectly well what she was doing when she went into that room with my best friend.

I *hate* hurting her and seeing her cry, but I stand firm on this shit.

"Jameson, please!" She grabs my face and yanks it so I'm looking down at her again. "Give me a chance to make it up to you. I'll prove to you that I can be trusted. I *love* you. I love you so damn much."

Grabbing the back of her head like I did earlier, I lean in close to her face and stop just inches from her lips. "Goodbye, Katie. Now get the fuck off my property."

With that, I remove her hand from my face and walk inside the house, leaving her outside to let it all sink in.

We're done and there's nothing she can do or say to change that. Just like there's nothing I can say or do to change the fact that she fucked my best friend.

Rowdy meets me at the door with a bottle of Jack, knowing damn well what I need at a time like this.

"Here you go, man. Get fucked up and I'll take care of the party." He grabs my shoulder and squeezes it, as I walk toward the staircase. "You deserve to drown in whiskey so I'll sober my ass up. For you."

Grabbing the bottle from Rowdy, I tilt it back, while making my way up the stairs and to my room.

I'm going to need more than just this bottle to numb the pain I'm feeling right now.

This is going to be a long night . . .

CHAPTER TWO

Two Weeks Later . . .
Jameson

THE CLUB IS PACKED TONIGHT, causing me to keep my guard up and my eyes open for drunken assholes, looking for a fight.

One fuck up and they're out.

Touch any woman in this room wrong or even give them a disrespectful look and I'll be on their ass so fucking fast that they won't even know it until they're out the door, with my knee in their neck.

I'm still on edge over the fact that Cole decided to take his job here back, knowing damn well that I still can't stand the sight of his ass.

I've still been picturing them together, thinking of all the ways I can rip his damn throat out for laying his hands on my girl and touching her in places only I should've been.

That's what him being here does. It allows more scenarios to fuck with my head, intensifying my hate for him.

It's been haunting me, making me want nothing more than to make him feel just a small bit of the pain he fucking made me feel and to let him know what it feels like to be stabbed in the back by the person you trust the most.

I've tried to move on, but I can't. Words can't fix the damage Cole did.

He's across the club, working the back section, but I've had my eye on him, watching him as he flirts with some dark-haired chick.

She's been coming here for the last week since Cole came back, so I can only assume she's here for him.

The animal inside of me, has me wanting to get her alone so I can dig my claws into her and work my way under her skin before Cole gets in too deep with her.

I want to make his ass work for what he wants. He doesn't deserve to have it easy after the shit he pulled on me.

Releasing a frustrated breath, I pull my eyes away from his section of the club and focus back on section A, walking around and making my rounds.

Stopping up at the bar, I tap it to get Violet's attention, noticing that the guy in front of her hasn't given her space since he walked through the door an hour ago. "You good over here, V?"

Looking away from the bearded guy, Violet flashes me a quick smile and leans over to grab my face and press her red lips against my cheek. "I'm always good when your sexy ass is here to keep all the jerks in check. He's a friend, but thank you, Jameson." She makes a sad face and places her hand over mine for comfort, most likely noticing my expression. "Everything okay, honey? I heard about Katie. What a bitch. You're too hot for her anyway, babe. You'll find better."

I tense my jaw and look up at her, trying to keep my cool. "I guess news travels fast around here."

Fucking Rowdy.

"That's what happens when you're friends with Rowdy. He gets high and his sexy lips won't stop moving," she says with a small smile. "But I'm here if you need to talk. I've dated assholes like her before. I know what it takes to get over it and I'm willing to help."

"Thanks, babe." I grab her hand from mine and kiss it, wanting to keep things friendly between us. I have enough messes to clean up at this club. "Let me know if anyone gives you a hard time."

"Will do, babe."

Nodding my head, I leave her alone so I can scan the rest of the room out, keeping my eyes out for anyone who's had too much to drink.

After a while, I get bored, my eyes wandering back over to Cole's section to see that the girl he's been all over is walking through the crowd with one of her friends, heading toward the bathroom.

Cole seems to be busy, so I take this as my opportunity to get her to notice me, making my way through the crowd, ignoring all the other females on the way.

My focus is *her*.

The line to the restroom is long as usual, so she and her friend line up at the end, talking and laughing about something.

The closer I get to her, the more intrigued I become as I step around to the side and my eyes land on her face up close for the first time.

I freeze, unable to turn away as she looks away from her friend to look up at me. She's breathing heavily, fighting to catch her breath from all the dancing they've been doing.

Her long, wavy black hair and bright blue eyes, speak right to my dick, making it stand tall as my eyes roam over her curvy body.

Locking eyes with her, I lift a brow, checking her out, not hiding the fact that I find her attractive.

That's the first step to getting her interested. Curiosity always gets the best of women when it comes to me. Always has.

Tightening my jaw, I allow my eyes to land on her plump lips, before I lick my own and walk away.

I can feel her eyes on me, watching my every step as her friend laughs and tries to get her attention. "Brooke . . . bring it back to reality. You listening to me?"

Satisfied with her reaction to me, I stop Wendy as she walks by, carrying her shot tray. "I'll take those last two shots." I pull out a twenty and drop it on her tray, grabbing the blue shots.

"Sure thing, Jameson." She smiles and holds up the bill with a smirk. "Change?"

"Keep it."

By the time I turn back around, Brooke and her friend are practically standing right beside me now as the line slowly moves up. I can see her secretly checking me out, while her friend continues to talk about Cole, asking her about the sex and how well he can take care of her.

Perfect timing to step in.

Giving them a confident smile, I step into their space, handing them both a shot.

Without giving Brooke the chance to speak, I tangle my hand into the back of her hair and lean in to whisper in her ear, "I'll take care of you. I'm really fucking generous when it comes to women. Just ask my friend Cole." I smile as she leans in closer to my lips as if she wants to hear more. I clearly have her interest now. "Shots are on me."

She lets out a small breath when I pull away, but only offers me a smile as she tilts the shot back, keeping her eyes locked with mine. She seems a bit . . . *speechless.*

I'm still way too close to her personal space, when I look over to see Cole walking toward us.

He doesn't look the least bit pleased as his eyes catch mine, his muscles flexing with each step toward us.

Smirking, I push the ear piece further into my ear, when I hear Rowdy's voice come through, asking me to come watch the entrance door for him. It's a Saturday night so there's no way he'll be able to leave his spot without me filling in for him.

"Great fucking timing," I mumble to Cole, knowing that he can hear Rowdy calling for me.

"You're telling me," he grinds out, getting close to my ear. "Better hurry, Jameson. *I* can take care of my girl just fine. Let's not do this shit. I know where you're taking this."

We both look over to the sound of Brooke's voice. "Jameson . . ." she holds up the empty shot glass and smiles, while looking at my lips as if she wants to taste them. "Thanks for the shot. It was delicious."

"Mmm . . ." her friend wipes her mouth off and smiles up at me, looking satisfied and impressed. "Yes, thank you. It was so good."

"You're welcome, ladies."

Grabbing the back of Cole's head, I get in his face. "Then you know me well. Better hope you can take care of your girl just fine, *brother*. It would *suck* if she decides she wants us both to."

Looking over Cole's shoulder, I wink at Brooke, causing her face to turn red, before she leans in to whisper something in her friend's ear.

Cole's jaw clenches as he watches me grinning like an asshole.

"I think she likes me." My smile widens. "I guess we'll just have to see how much."

With that, I walk away, leaving Cole pissed off and probably thinking of all the ways he can keep me away from his girl, now that I've made it clear what's about to go down.

"Jameson, you dick." Rowdy throws the clipboard at my chest, giving me a hard look once I finally make it outside. "Took you long enough."

"Calm the fuck down. It's been five minutes. Your *client* can wait."

"This one doesn't." With that, Rowdy rushes through the parking lot, leaving me to watch the door so he can get high.

Between Cole being here and now dealing with Rowdy's shit, I'm itching to knock someone the fuck out.

I can only hope someone fucks up.

Pulling out a cigarette, I light it and stand back, watching the line full of people, just waiting for a reason to chase someone down.

I need something to get my adrenaline pumping and standing still does nothing but makes me antsy.

Usually, there's at least one idiot who thinks he can sneak his way into the club, without waiting to be let in.

"Jameson," Rev's voice comes through my ear piece, causing me to stand tall and listen. "We have another runner. Left out the back door of the poker room. You're going to love this one." He laughs. "I'm sending Serge to watch the door."

Smirking, I toss my cigarette down, before dropping the clipboard and taking off through the alley.

If it's not someone trying to sneak in, then it's someone trying to sneak out from downstairs.

Adrenaline has me running fast, rounding the corner, just in time to clothesline the idiot, stupid enough to think he can get away without paying his debt.

The guy hits the ground hard, coughing out as his breath gets knocked out of him.

This isn't the first time I've chased him down and I know it won't be the last. He should be banned by now, but I enjoy these moments too much.

Standing over him, I place my foot on his neck and call back to Rev.

"How much does James owe this time?"

Rev laughs into the ear piece. "Damn, that was faster than usual, man. Fifty-five hundred."

Removing my boot from James' neck, I roll him over and pull his wallet from his pocket. "Did you really think it was going to be that easy to get away, James?" I empty the cash from his wallet, tossing the leather down on his chest.

"Yeah . . . thought you were off tonight. Guess I was wrong." He coughs and sits up, watching as I count his money. "I don't have enough cash right now. It's why I ran."

"No shit," I mumble, while grabbing his arm and taking off his watch. "Guess this shit will do."

"It better," he says, while standing up and smoothing out his suit. "That's a Rolex. It's worth way more than I owe."

"Well, consider it a down payment for the next time you run then, asshole." I slap his chest and back up. "Cause we all know I'll catch you again. I'm beginning to like this little relationship we have."

Winking, I turn around and head back to the club, feeling just a tiny bit better now that I've had some action.

Damn, I needed this. I'll have to remember to thank James someday for giving me someone to take my aggression out on . . .

Hard and Reckless is Available Now

Read on for the first two chapters of AFFLICTION by Jenika Snow

AFFLICTION
CHAPTER ONE

THE SWEAT RUNNING DOWN THE valley between my breasts was reminiscent of fingers moving along me. I was hot, my body flushed, my heart racing. Everything in me felt alive, ready to tear through my skin like another entity wanting to escape.

I was drunk, and I felt incredible.

The bodies pressed tightly against me, moving sexually, suggestively, made me feel even better. It made me feel alive. I moved with them, swaying to the music, inhaling the scent of sex and alcohol that seemed to surround me.

I was sure a lot of people would be fucking tonight. No doubt it would be dirty, their inhibitions having been left at the club as they took home a random person. It would be the kind of sex that drunk people had, sloppy, carefree.

I wasn't a good girl. I didn't follow the rules. And my life was less than memorable. I lived like today was my last, because for all I knew it would be. It could be.

I came to this club when I couldn't stand the box that was my life, the one that was sealed tight, no airholes, no light getting through the crack. I got wasted, danced until my body was covered with sweat, my muscles sore, and some poor, hard-up frat guy got off in his jeans by grinding against my leg.

I was a wreck in many ways, and I had no doubt that people assumed I was slutty by the way I dressed, by the way I moved on the dance floor.

But how I dressed and acted didn't make up who I was: a virgin who was lost, who had no one, nothing. I was an inexperienced woman who came here and danced because I wanted a little bit of release...the only kind I ever got.

How I felt here was like being consumed by the water, of being helpless but weightless, of being sucked down to the very bottom where no light was permitted.

I wasn't light. I was darkness wrapped up in a five-foot-five frame, with dark hair, a wild streak, and no one to stop me.

Maybe I was a contradiction to myself, a lost girl who didn't know what she wanted in life. But it's who I was, how I got through each day.

I embraced it, knowing that maybe my upbringing made me this way, that having an absentee mother, a drunk for a father, and a penchant for getting slapped on occasion by said parents had shaped the woman I now was.

I wasn't broken, but I was damaged.

Or maybe it had nothing to do with my parents or what I didn't have growing up: love. Maybe I was just born this way.

Either way I didn't try and stop it. I didn't try and change.

"You look good out here dancing, girl." The feeling of a guy behind me, of his hands on my hips, his hard cock digging into my lower back, had dual sensations moving through me. "You feel good," he said again, his voice thick, aroused, slurred from the no doubt many drinks he'd consumed. "What's your name?"

I thought about lying, pretending I was someone else. Instead

I said, "Sofia."

The truth.

I wanted him to get off, because knowing I had that kind of control, that kind of power, fueled me. But on the other hand I felt disgust, mainly for myself. I felt and smelled his hot, liquor-laced breath along my neck. I shivered, and the way he groaned made me assume he thought it meant I was into this.

I wasn't, but I didn't stop from grinding on him.

I lifted my hands, closed my eyes, and just thought about something else. I wasn't here, wasn't trying to get this guy to come in his pants. I was far away, so distant that nothing could touch me. I was the one who had control, and that control made me feel free, alive.

"Come home with me. Hell, let's go back to my car."

I shook my head. He needed to shut up.

"Come on, girl." He ground his dick against me again. He felt small, even though he was hard.

"No. Either shut up and dance with me, or go find someone willing to go home with you." I didn't even know if he heard me over the rush of the music, but if he said one more word, I'd just go get a drink.

He tightened his hold on my hips, digging his small dick into my back. "I bet you're wet for me right now, aren't you?" His breath was hot, humid. It was acidic and I gagged.

I was bone-dry, not even the teasing of arousal playing over me. I never felt anything when I danced with these guys. It was what made me feel free, made me feel powerful in an otherwise unstable world.

I might not have any kind of control with my personal life, with my finances, with anything that could ground me, but at this club, where the drinks flowed, the sex was potent, and my power was immense...I was the one in charge.

I'd been called a dick tease, a bitch, whore, a cunt...any and all of the above. None of that mattered. They were verbal bullets, and in this club I wore my bulletproof vest.

I pushed away from the guy and made my way to the bar. He was either cursing me out or had hopefully moved on to someone more receptive to what he was actually after. But when I got to the bar, the people crammed together, shouting, lifting their hands to get one of the three bartenders to come their way.

I decided tonight was done. I'd hit the bathroom, then call a cab.

Pushing my way through the throng of bodies, the air stale, humid, the heat suffocating, I said a silent prayer that the line to use the bathroom wasn't up the ass. But there were still a few girls ahead of me.

I leaned on the wall, resting my head back against it, and stared up. I noticed the video camera aimed right at me. There were several in this hallway, two in the back, one pointing at me, and another aimed at the dance floor.

I had no doubt there were a dozen more at other locations. Although this place was wild on most nights, it also had a reputation for being safe—well, as safe as a nightclub could be. It had just been renovated by the new owner over the last year, a man I'd heard rumors about, and one I never wanted to meet.

Dark and dangerous. Violent and psychotic. He's not a person you want to meet in a dark alley. He'd just as soon slit your throat for looking at him the wrong way.

Rumors, of course, but it was those words, whispered by everyone and anyone, that told me there had to be a little bit of truth behind them.

I feel sorry for anyone who pisses off Cameron Ashton, because he'll solve that problem with a shovel and a six-foot-deep hole.

Pushing off the wall when it was my turn inside, I used the facility, went over to the sink to wash my hands, and stared at myself in the mirror. The girl who stared back looked sad, and not in an emotional way. My reflection showed a hot mess.

My eyeliner was starting to smear under my eyes, pieces of my dark hair stuck to my temples, and the lipstick I had on, once red and vibrant, now looked dead and colorless.

I finished in the restroom, pushed my way through the crowd, and finally opened the door that led outside. The cool night air washed over me, and I involuntarily closed my eyes, moaning softly. It felt good out here, the crush of bodies and heat a distant memory the longer I stood here.

The alcohol that had once numbed me, clouding my head with the nothingness, started to clear. Maybe I hadn't been as drunk as I'd thought. Being behind those doors was like another world. The lights, music, the people trying to get off any way they could, brought you down low to a depraved, sticky and disgusting level. It's what I loved.

I needed to get home now, had work in the morning, had to get back to my shitty life. I fished my cell out of the minuscule handbag I carried with me, dialed the cab service I had memorized, and told them the address.

Coming here for the last year should have had them knowing me by name. As I waited for them to arrive, ten long fucking minutes, I moved away from the front doors and leaned against the wall off to the side.

I glanced up, the streetlight close by bright but not quite reaching me fully. Looking to my left, I noticed another security camera, this one pointed at the front doors. Never let it be said this place didn't have their shit together.

The sound of a lighter going off to my right had me glancing over. I saw the flare of the flame, smelled the scent of the cigarette as its owner inhaled and then exhaled.

"Hey, girl."

I exhaled. God, of course the guy from inside, the one with the small dick and the need for me to go home with him, would be out here. I didn't bother replying, didn't want to engage. Instead I turned my head in the other direction and glanced at a few people across the parking lot smoking. I felt the lightest touch on my arm.

The hell?

I glanced to my right, and before I knew what was happening, that light touch from the asshole turned into him pulling me farther into the shadowy side street.

CHAPTER TWO

"HEY," I SHOUTED, BUT HE clapped his hand over my mouth. Panic welled in me so violently I couldn't think straight. My heart started hammering against my ribs when he pushed me farther into the shadowy abyss.

He had me pinned to the side of the wall, the brick scraping along my back. There'd be marks on my flesh, but that was the least of my worries. His forearm on my throat cut off my oxygen. I clawed at his arm, my nails digging at his skin. He hissed and put more pressure on my neck.

My head started to grow fuzzy, my body going numb. I was far beyond panicking, the survival instinct rising up violently.

"You stupid fucking cunt," he said close to my face, his breath smelling stale, the aroma of the cigarette he'd been smoking making me sick to my stomach. I would have thrown up, but the struggle to breathe everything us being cut off.

The sound of a belt buckle being undone, of a zipper being pulled down, brought reality crashing down on me. I wouldn't be able to get out of this, not without a hell of a lot more damage than just the scrapes on my back. The sound of people coming in and out of the club was so close, yet so far away.

"You should have taken me up on my offer to come back to my place. I would have been gentle with you."

Lies.

"But now you'll get fucked in this dirty alley like the whore you are."

I felt his erection against my belly. I tried to say something, to yell out, do anything that would make me more than a victim waiting to get attacked.

The flash of headlights pulling into the alley had my attacker stilling and glancing to the side. He kept his forearm on my throat but tucked himself back into his pants. He moved closer to me so I had no doubt that whoever was in that car couldn't see his arm pressing into me, cutting off my oxygen.

It was clear he didn't care or was too drunk to have a problem with someone seeing us in this position. But I supposed it might look like two people about to get it on...both consenting, even though I wanted to knee this fucker in the balls.

"Make one sound and I'll find out where you live, come in through your window, and really do some damage."

No way in hell I'd take his threat seriously, even if he meant one word. This would be my only chance to get help. Because even if I did nothing, he'd still destroy me.

The car was a good ten feet away, and the headlights were shining right on us, the vehicle just idling now. It seemed like forever before the sound of a door opening and closing came, louder than the rush of conversation from the club goers just around the corner. I heard feet hitting pavement in an easy, relaxed pace; then the sight of a large body—very large—came into view. I could only assume it was a man, given the size. He stayed behind the lights, the shadows wrapping around his tall frame.

He stared at us for long seconds, and for some reason all I could do was stare right back. My reality came into view and I started to struggle. I caught the asshole holding me off guard and managed to push him back enough that his forearm was no longer pressed painfully into my throat.

I sucked in oxygen, sweet, life-sustaining oxygen. My throat burned, and a flush stole over me, the pain of being able to breathe again claiming me.

"You fucking bitch," the asshole next to me hissed.

And then there was the sound of another door opening and closing, of a gun being cocked. The shadowy man tipped his head to the side, the air around him seeming charged, electric. It was the slightest move, but it caused whoever had just gotten out of the car to start walking toward us.

"The fuck?" the asshole pinned against me said in a hushed voice, his eyes squinted, the headlights blinding us. I feared the worst, thinking maybe I'd misjudged whoever had shown up as being able to help. Maybe they were worse than the fucker who'd attacked me.

And then the guy was pulled away from me, the sweet relief of his body no longer on mine urging me to run. But I was frozen in place, the dark shapes still covered in the shadows, the headlights still blinding me, making it impossible to see anything clearly. I rubbed my throat, the burn almost unbearable. And then a body was thrown against the side of the building, and I realized it was my attacker.

I stood there shocked, unable to move, as I watched a man approach. His body was illuminated by the intense yellow glow of his headlights. But his face was still concealed. An air of danger came from this man like a punch to my gut. I sucked in more oxygen, this time not having anything to do with the fact it was difficult to breathe.

I stared at the man currently holding the attacker asshole up against the brick wall by his neck. Whoever the man was, he was big, supporting another human as if it was nothing at all. I covered my chest, despite the fact that I was dressed. It was like my secrets were exposed.

When I glanced at the man who'd tilted his head, who'd sent his guard dog to do his bidding I knew he was watching me. I might not be able to see his face, but I felt his eyes on me like fingers touching me, stroking me, holding me down.

And then my heart seized in my chest as I watched him lift his arm, the gun I'd heard being cocked most likely the one he held. He was right next to the body pinned to the wall. The guy was struggling to breathe, clawing at the grip the man had on his throat.

Just like me. A taste of his own medicine.

He kept moving closer to the man pinned to the wall, but I knew he watched me, knew he was calculating all of this. I thought I'd be able to see him when he moved away from the headlights, once they weren't blocking the front of him. But when he was standing next to his partner or guard dog or whatever the hell the guy was to him, I still couldn't make out his face.

I knew I wouldn't have known him anyway, but I wanted to look into the face of the man who'd saved me.

Saved me?

Yes, he'd saved me from a very dark hole, pulled me out so I could breathe again. But I now had this feeling, this sensation like honey on my skin, thick, almost suffocating me again, that this man was far more dangerous than anything I'd ever come across.

He said nothing, and the only sound that penetrated my foggy brain was of the man struggling, of his wheezes and gasps as he tried to claw at the hand holding him, keeping him up. I felt nothing, no sympathy for him, nothing but the need to see him hurt the way he'd hurt me.

And then, my lungs clenching painfully with every inhalation I made, I watched the man push away his partner and take his place in front of my attacker. Instinct, survival told me to run, to get the hell out of here because this was going straight into hell, where the flames licked at me, threatening to burn me alive.

The man had his head turned in my direction, the fucking shadows making him seem almost unreal, like maybe this was all a hallucination. He was so big, taller, thicker, and more muscular than the man pressed to the wall in front of him. Still he stayed silent; still he watched me. And then he lifted his hand, placed the barrel of the gun against my attacker's forehead, right in the damn center, and everything seemed to stand still.

I knew enough about guns, had seen plenty of movies, to know the silencer attached would make this clean, would have no one panicking and rushing away at the sound of a gunshot.

I took a step forward, not sure why I'd do that. It was the equivalent of trying to touch a chained, starved dog, wanting to run my hands over it even though I knew it would attack me, tear me from limb to limb.

"No," I said. He might have been about to attack me, rape me, God, who knew what else, but I didn't want him to die. I couldn't stand here and watch some man shoot him. I couldn't live with myself with that hanging over me, even if he deserved that and more. "No. Wait," I whispered. A long moment passed, maybe a second, maybe an hour. It seemed like ages where my body was stiff, my heart thundering, the man with the gun staring at me. He didn't pull the trigger, even though maybe he should have. I felt dizzy, my head swimming, the feeling of falling having nothing to do with the drinks I'd had or the situation that had transpired up until right now. "It's not worth it. He's not worth it," I whispered again, but even though I didn't know this man, I knew that he wasn't the type to give a shit about what was worth it or not. He did what he did because he wanted to.

I knew that as well as I knew the man with the gun pointed to his head could be shot dead at any second.

I was very aware of the blood rushing through my veins, drowning everything else out. The frat guy was saying something, but I couldn't hear it, couldn't focus on anything but the man in front of me who held so much power it could have brought me to my knees.

After a tense second he took a step back, the gun still in his hand, his focus now on the asshole who'd had me in a choke hold. He still hadn't said one word, not when he cocked the weapon, and not when he had his thug slam the frat-guy up against the building. And he didn't say anything when he lifted his arm and rammed the butt of the gun at the asshole's temple. The guy slid to the ground, maybe knocked out, maybe trying to make himself smaller, less noticeable.

And then there was nothing but him and me, staring at each other, the air thick, the world washing away. He turned and left me standing there, his hand at his side, the gun still in his grasp. The flash of a ring caught my attention, a thick one wrapped around his pinky, seeming much more ominous than it should.

He got back in the car and drove off. I followed the car with my gaze, watching it disappear down the road, knowing he was staring at me the same as I was him.

I had no idea what in the hell had happened.

I didn't know if I'd ever be the same.

AFFLICTION is Available Now

VICTORIA ASHLEY

VICTORIA ASHLEY GREW UP IN Rockford, IL and has had a passion for reading for as long as she can remember. After finding a reading app where it allowed readers to upload their own stories, she gave it a shot and writing became her passion.

She lives for a good romance book with tattooed bad boys that are just highly misunderstood and is not afraid to be caught crying during a good read. When she's not reading or writing about bad boys, you can find her watching her favorite shows such as Supernatural, Sons Of Anarchy and The Walking Dead.

Contact her at:
www.victoriaashleyauthor.com
www.facebook.com/VictoriaAshleyAuthor
Twitter: @VictoriaAauthor
Intstagram: VictoriaAshley.Author

BOOKS BY VICTORIA ASHLEY

WALK OF SHAME SERIES
Slade (Book 1)
Hemy (Book 2)
Cale (Book 3)

WALK OF SHAME 2ND GENERATION SERIES
Stone (Book 1)
Styx (Book 2)

SAVAGE & INK SERIES
Royal Savage (Book 1)

THE PAIN SERIES
Get Off On the Pain (Book 1)
Something For the Pain (Book 2)

STAND ALONE TITLES
Wake Up Call
This Regret
Thrust

BOOKS CO-WRITTEN WITH HILARY STORM
ALPHACHAT.COM SERIES
Pay For Play (Book 1)
Two Can Play (Book 2)

JENIKA SNOW

JENIKA SNOW IS A USA Today bestselling Author of romance. She's a mother, wife, and nurse, and has been published since 2009. When not writing she can be found enjoying gloomy, rain-filled days, and wearing socks year-round.

Contact her at:
www.JenikaSnow.com
www.facebook.com/jenikasnow
Twitter: @jenikasnow
Intstagram: @jenikasnow

You can find more information on all her titles at:
www.JenikaSnow.com

ACKNOWLEDGMENTS

VICTORIA ASHLEY

FIRST AND FOREMOST, I'D LIKE to say a HUGE thank you to Jenika Snow for taking a chance and writing this amazing story with me.

I'd also like to thank the beta readers that took the time to read Pay for Play: Lindsey and Amy. We appreciate you ladies so much!

Lea Schafer for doing a wonderful job at editing and Dana Leah for her amazing design work on our cover.

And I want to say a big thank you to all of my loyal readers that have given me support over the last couple of years and have encouraged me to continue with my writing. Your words have all inspired me to do what I enjoy and love. Each and every one of you mean a lot to me and I wouldn't be where I am if it weren't for your support and kind words.

Last but not least, I'd like to thank all of the wonderful book bloggers that have taken the time to support our book and help spread the word. You all do so much for us authors and it is greatly appreciated. I have met so many friends on the way and you guys are never forgotten. You guys rock. Thank you!

JENIKA SNOW

A BIG THANK YOU TO Victoria for going on this adventure with me and creating dark and twisted characters that we love to hate! This story wouldn't be possible without the help from so many people: Dana, our cover designer, Lindsey, who took the time to go over the story and give us her opinion, Lea Ann, who is an incredible editor, Ardent Prose for their help in promoting, and of course all the readers and bloggers who support our crazy endeavors.

.

Made in the USA
Las Vegas, NV
24 July 2021

27003506R00105